WITHDRAWN

The Dream

David J Bailey

instant
apostle

First published in Great Britain in 2018

Instant Apostle

The Barn
1 Watford House Lane
Watford
Herts
WD17 1BJ

British Library Cataloguing-in-Publication Data

A catalogue record for this book is available from the British Library

This book and all other Instant Apostle books are available from
Instant Apostle:

Website: www.instantapostle.com
E-mail: info@instantapostle.com

ISBN 978-1-909728-77-6

Printed in Great Britain

Editor's note for young readers

This is a work of fiction and the children in the story have wonderful adventures with people they don't know, who turn out to be angels! *But, remember, this is only a story.* In real life, we must never trust strangers and go off with them, however amazing and angelic they seem!

Also, while Oliver and Jess receive their hearts' desire in a splendid and unforeseen way, we need to remember that although God is a God of miracles, He doesn't *always* make our dreams come true in quite such a spectacular fashion! However, that doesn't mean He can't do great things for us, and faith can achieve much. Trust God! He loves you, He truly wants to bless you and He wants His best for you. Remember, though: God's best may not be what we consider best, but He knows us better than we know ourselves.

About the author

David J Bailey is married to Gillian, with three grown-up children and six grandchildren. After a career in engineering and later as a Baptist minister, he retired in 2005. Writing has always been his passion.

Cover images: © candy1812, © lizabarbiza, © twindesigner, all AdobeStock.
Cover design by Jude May Design.

Contents

1. Oliver's World

Oliver Carrick's day at school had, he felt, hit rock bottom. It had been a terrible day; bullying was a daily routine for him, but today had been worse than ever. Teachers had accused him of being aggressive because he had retaliated with his fists against two of the bullies. He could never have hoped to win a fist fight with either of them, but he'd had enough and decided it was time to take action; unfortunately, he chose a moment when a teacher was passing and accordingly he was hauled over the coals and given a week-long detention.

No one wanted to hear his side of things, so he was branded the bully – him, Oliver the 'wimp', Oliver the 'mummy's boy', Oliver the 'princess'. He hoped that when he got home his mum would be alone and he could pour out his heart to her, but, in fact, when he got there her latest partner, for no apparent reason, also thrashed him and sent him up to his room without any tea. Oliver was a mess; he felt completely unloved, friendless and alone. He went to bed hungry and without any contact with his mum. That night he cried himself to sleep. He was totally distraught and desperate for love, support, protection – someone to care, but there was no one.

That night Oliver had a dream, a nightmare: he was in a strange house and he was upstairs in one of three bedrooms; he was not aware of anyone else in the house, yet he sensed a presence and he began to feel very frightened. He was in bed, so he pulled the covers right over his head, but the presence, the fear, the feelings of desperation didn't go away; rather, they intensified. Eventually he could stand it no longer and he threw off the covers, jumped out of bed and dashed from the room. As he crossed the landing he was aware that something or someone was bearing down on him, so he flew down the stairs, his feet barely touching the steps, dashed through a door at the bottom and quickly slammed it behind him. Here he felt safe. At that precise moment he awoke and, although he knew it was only a dream, a terrible nightmare, even, the feeling of fear and horror remained. How he longed for his mum to hold him and reassure him as she had when he was little, but now he didn't dare even cry out for fear of the consequences.

Oliver was thirteen years old and lived with his mum, Jenny, and... dad? Well, not exactly: to date he'd had six dads, none of whom was his birth father, Peter. He believed his mother loved him, but she was not allowed to show love or tenderness towards him. Her numerous partners had initially shown him some care, but all too soon he became the nuisance, the one who was in the way and not wanted. Violence was often meted out without cause, and eventually, when Oliver was covered in cuts and bruises, his mother would send her boyfriends packing, but this was not so with Jez – or at least, if she'd tried, he refused to leave and used his fists to impose his determination to stay.

Oliver had been a very sickly baby and toddler, suffering one illness after another; consequently, he was physically underdeveloped and looked very young for his age. He was small in stature and skinny in the extreme. It was because of this, together with his lack of strength, that everyone picked on him – he was ripe for the bullying regime. It was a state of affairs that simply got worse as time went by, and now it seemed no one sided with him, not even others who were experiencing bullying. Life at school was unbearable and his grades suffered accordingly, but teachers' reports said that he lacked self-discipline and his concentration seemed to be sadly lacking. Nothing, in fact, could have been further from the truth, and if he'd been allowed to be a normal boy and free from being terrorised, he could have achieved much higher grades – he loved learning and had an inquisitive mind that longed to be fed. Instead, he was branded a loser, and nothing he did could dispel that image.

Every night for the next couple of weeks the same dream recurred, and every night he awoke feeling the same fear, longing and desperation, but no one cared. He was entirely alone. If only his real dad was around! He felt sure he'd have been loved by him and he would have listened and cared. Oliver knew his mum was desperate for love too; deep down she was hurting – she hadn't said so, but Oliver could see it in her eyes even when she was in the company of her latest partner.

What Oliver didn't know was that Jenny had witnessed his homecoming from school – clearly deeply distressed – and she hurt inside. Also, whenever he was being ill-treated by the latest man in her life, she longed to protect him, to hold him tight and show him some tenderness, but she knew only too well what she'd suffer if she made a move to comfort him. She struggled to stand up for herself, having suffered a severe mental breakdown when she lost a baby she was expecting, and then her husband, Peter, walked out on them. Now she needed a man for financial support. She feared what would happen to Oliver, but her dependence was stronger than her maternal instinct. How she wished that Peter had never left. He was a rock and very dependable. He really had loved them all and life had been great...

Over the next couple of weeks, things at school deteriorated still further; the bullying got worse and Oliver began to behave badly, just in the hope that he'd get some attention and someone, just for once, would notice his desperate plight. Detentions came thick and fast; the school sent letters to his mum, but when Oliver saw the unopened letters on the floor behind the front door, he tore them up and binned them.

Eventually the inevitable happened and he was excluded for a week for violence towards the teaching staff. It was a most unlikely scenario, because Oliver's stature didn't correspond with his behaviour. However, instead of noticing this, the school took everything at face value. Oliver was glad, as he could leave the house each morning as normal and do his own thing each day without anyone being any the wiser. He began to target the local shops, stealing to feed his hunger and to gratify the anger he felt towards everyone.

It was the disturbed nights that left him acutely tired and contributed to his behavioural problems, because once awake, he dare not go to sleep again in case the nightmare recurred. Inevitably, even though he tried to stay awake, he eventually did fall asleep, but then one night he dreamed he was standing outside that strange house, simply looking at it. Thoughts entered his sleeping mind that the house was real, that it did exist and somehow he had to find it. So, far from being a house of fear, it somehow held the key to his happiness – but how that could be, when it had always been a house of dread, a house where danger lurked and pursuit awaited, he just could not comprehend.

The next morning he again had to pretend to get ready for school. His mum and her partner were not up, so Oliver helped himself to a good breakfast of dry toast, washed down with water. He packed a few extra slices of bread in a plastic bag and thrust them into his pocket. Just then, he heard the others stirring, so he quickly grabbed his coat and dashed from the house before he could get the obligatory slap.

It was a bright early summer's morning, cool but promising warmth to come. There was a wonderful sense of freedom in the open air, as if all were well in his world. If all really was well he'd be enjoying the walk to school with fellow pupils, but Oliver set off in the opposite direction, unsure of where he was going or how he was going to spend the day. He came to a newsagent and walked in with the other early morning customers, grabbed a couple of chocolate bars and a can of fizzy drink and walked calmly out among the other shoppers. He knew stealing was wrong, but this was, he felt, a much-needed treat. He walked on and crossed a large plot of waste ground that was shortly due for development. He'd been here before and he knew that there was a dilapidated brick building on the site. It was dirty, smelly and probably rat-infested, but it did afford some shelter from prying eyes and a place to sit and think. Thinking was something he felt he must do after that latest dream.

Even now, as he recalled the dream, he felt certain that the house he kept seeing was somehow real, and he increasingly felt it was drawing him towards it. Why did it intrigue him so? It had been a place he'd hated night after night, so why should it be any different now, and if he should find it, would it fulfil his desires or would his life be in danger?

'I don't want to go there,' his mind screamed out. 'I don't want to find it, I don't want to encounter that... whatever it was!'

What was it or who was it that always chased him, always tried to swallow him up? Was it some dreadful monster, some awful fiend, or was it someone with evil intentions?

'I don't want to find out, I don't want to go there; I'm not going and that's final!' These thoughts, these arguments were playing out in his mind. So why was it continually pestering him this way? It was that dream, that latest dream; it seemed to be saying that that house held many answers, the key to happiness for him. He really didn't have a choice; he did have to find it.

'Not today, though,' he reasoned. 'Another day.'

He didn't even know where it was, so how could he go there? Where would he start? No, another day, another day would be best – a day when things were clearer. A good thought came to him. Surely, he'd know when it was *that* day and it certainly wasn't today.

That evening at the appropriate time, the time he would normally arrive home from school, he walked in through the front door and was met by Jez.

'Hello, Oliver,' he greeted the boy in a friendly tone of voice. 'Have you had a good day at school? What did you learn about today?'

Oliver was immediately on his guard. Never before had Jez asked him about school, and he'd never spoken to him in that friendly tone. Something, he feared, was very wrong – just what was coming? This was most certainly the calm before the storm, because this was Jez speaking and Jez didn't do nice, he didn't do friendliness – well, not to Oliver, anyway.

'Er... er... yeah, it was all right, a bit boring at times, and...'

Before he could say anything more, the storm struck. 'You're a lying little toad, you haven't been to school and I know because the school have been on to us – you've been suspended for violence against the teachers. You horrible little urchin, I'll teach you to tell lies – you'll not do so again when I've finished with you!'

The first blow crashed into his left ear and sent him reeling across the room. He was then grabbed by his shirt-front, hauled to his feet and slapped right, left and centre. Slowly Oliver felt his breath knocked from his body and a thick darkness began to descend. He finally crashed to the floor in a lifeless heap. He had a vague recollection of a violent kick to his ribs and then someone yelling for Jez to stop.

Stop it he did, as far as Oliver was concerned, but Jez's venom was not yet spent, and Oliver's eyes were just able to discern his mum getting a violent punch to her face. Sheer anger surged in his previously spent body and a rush of adrenaline forced him to his feet; he had to stop his mum from receiving a battering, so grabbing a chair, he swung it with all the force he could muster. Jez had just turned as the chair headed towards him and his left arm took the full force. Snorting like a bull in a rage, he aimed a savage blow with his other fist at Oliver's jaw. Oliver anticipated it and tried to ride the punch, but it still landed with sufficient force to knock him senseless.

It was pitch black when he regained consciousness and he found himself fully clothed, sprawled across his bed, where he'd obviously been dumped. His head throbbed, his jaw felt like it had been hit with a sledgehammer; he was battered and bruised all over. He could taste blood, so he crept to the bathroom and washed his mouth and bathed his face. He found some painkillers in the bathroom cabinet and swallowed a couple. The others he put in his pocket in case he needed more, and then he returned to his room. He sank onto his bed and was soon fast asleep, only to dream once again.

He saw that same house, but he didn't stop and go inside; he walked on by and came to a park, where he sat on a bench. The park was deserted, but then suddenly a big man approached. At first he expected it to be Jez, but this man was smiling and friendly, and sat down beside him.

After a few moments, the man spoke.

'Hello, you must be Oliver.'

'Yes, I am, but who are you?'

'I'm just a messenger. I have been sent to give you a message: you are hurting desperately and you long for help and comfort; well, know this, your cry has been heard and help is at hand. Tomorrow you will walk, seemingly aimlessly, but in your wanderings you will meet a woman dressed in yellow. Go with her, she will help you on your journey to peace and happiness. You will meet with her at exactly 9.00am. You have to go and find that house you see in your dreams. For the next stage of your journey you will need to go to St Martin's Church, where you will meet a man who will care for you and point you towards your next destination. Ask for directions to the church from the woman in yellow and she will help you.'

The dream faded and when Oliver awoke next it was light, but still very early, and no one in the house was yet stirring. He got up, washed and dressed, applied some soothing cream he'd found in the bathroom cabinet to his bruised face, and crept quietly downstairs. He was not going to stay and be battered again. He had thought about going and battering Jez while he slept, but had decided not to sink to Jez's level – anyway, his mum would suffer for his actions and he wasn't going to inflict that on her. No, the best thing was to get as far away as possible, and anyway, he had to meet the woman in yellow.

He laughed to himself at that thought. Of course he wouldn't meet such a person – it was only a dream. He gobbled down a quick breakfast of toast and packed the rest of the loaf in a rucksack, together with a chunk of cheese and an apple. He found a bottle of water in the fridge and put that in too. He had a last look round the room and finally noticed Jez's phone on a shelf; he decided to grab that and as he did so found a £5 note and pocketed that too. He put on his shoes and crept out of the back door, closing it silently behind him. He walked into the rear alleyway and made his way to the main road. He was free, well clear of Jez's prying eyes; if he never saw him again it would be too soon.

He turned into the main road and headed towards the town; where he was going and what he would do, he really had no idea; at this precise moment that didn't matter – he simply wanted to get far away, and he could think about a plan of action later. Of course, the woman in yellow might come to his rescue. He smiled to himself, though smiling hurt his swollen face; it was nonsense to think that a dream could have any significance or could become reality. Believing such a possibility would, he reasoned, be just another thing to be teased and bullied about; no, dreams were private, something best kept to oneself – they were rubbish anyway.

Try as he might, though, the thoughts kept coming – what if it really did happen, what if the woman was real and did suddenly appear? No, no, no, dreams don't come true. He refused to believe that there was even the remotest possibility. 'But what if… OK, I'll see what happens when that precise time comes; it's only 6.45 now, so two and a quarter hours to go.' Still smiling, despite the pain, he began to sing the Liverpool anthem: 'My team – come on you Reds.' He continued to hum the song for quite some time as he aimlessly walked the streets – as far as he was concerned, going nowhere in particular.

The streets were getting busier now and newsagents were already open. He went into one and spent half of the £5 on crisps and chocolate, which he put into his rucksack. So, onwards he walked, and no one seemed to give him a second glance; many were rushing to catch buses or to get to work on time. He came to the bus station, so he turned in and found a seat in the waiting room; he ate a packet of crisps while he watched the people pass by.

'They're just like ants,' he thought to himself. 'Dashing here and there, seemingly without purpose – I wonder where they're all going? Hmm, why can't those coming from that direction save time and energy by doing what those coming from the other direction are going to do? Both lots could change their jobs. Some of them, I reckon, are just like me, they don't know where they're going nor why they're going there. Well, actually, no, I do know I have to find that house; I'm going there – that's where I'm going, but where is "there"? What am I thinking – *it was a dream*! Dreams don't become reality – I think the beating has addled my brain.'

He stayed there thinking for quite some time and then decided to move on. He wondered, 'Shall I go left or right?' He took a coin from his pocket. 'Heads I go right and tails I go left.' It was heads, so that was the way he turned, and he walked steadily on for quite some distance. He looked at his watch again, 8.45, only a quarter of an hour to go. 'Then I'll see what games the mind can play; I know it was all rubbish, so I expect nothing. I've often had strange thoughts in the past and thank goodness most of them were not real.'

2. Marianne

By now, Oliver was leaving the town centre behind; he found himself walking through the suburbs. 'How far am I going to aimlessly walk? I'll have to decide on a plan soon – I think that stuff about the house is just my imagination.'

It was nearly nine o'clock, so Oliver stopped and counted down the seconds – half a minute, fifteen seconds, five, four, three, two, one – time! He looked around. 'There, I knew it, just a load of rubbish, so now what?'

'Hello, Oliver Carrick! You've come, then. I knew you would.'

The voice behind him was the loveliest he'd ever heard; he swung round, and standing there was a woman in a yellow coat. Not just any woman, but one who had the most beautiful face in the whole wide world, a face that seemed to somehow glow, and a smile that seemed to light everything up around her.

'Wowee! I… er… er… I mean… who are you? How do you know me and what do you want with me? I just don't believe this is real, I'm still dreaming aren't I? You're not real, are you?'

The woman chuckled. 'Yes, I'm real, Oliver, and no, you're not dreaming. Take my hand and know that I have substance just like you.'

Oliver tentatively took her outstretched hand; the moment their hands met, he felt warmth spread through his whole body; a gentle tingling sensation that totally removed all feeling of the severe beating that Jez had meted out. He felt healthier, more alive, even, than he'd ever felt before. Strangely, he felt no fear; he was completely at ease and content to hold that hand for as long as he could. Although the woman did nothing but hold his hand, Oliver felt as though he was being embraced, loved and comforted as never before – the very experience he'd longed for throughout his young life. This woman was somehow the most wonderful mother *and* father all rolled into one. How he wished this moment could last forever.

They started to walk together, just a gentle pace. Oliver knew it was never right to go off with strangers, but somehow this was… different, she was different; instinctively he knew he could trust her and she meant him no harm – it was, he felt, an extension of his dream sequence.

'Where are we going? Where are you taking me? What are we going to do?' Oliver asked.

'Today I'm going to care for you, and after a good night's sleep I'll send you off on the next stage of your journey,' that gentle, caring voice replied.

'Journey, what journey? Where am I supposed to be going?'

She chuckled again. 'You know, Oliver… you know you have to find that house. I sense you're feeling very relaxed at this moment in time, but it's only when you find that house that you'll be truly happy, content and fulfilled. It's worth all the seeking, so no matter what you have to face, don't give up on the quest; you will get there and then you'll know and then you'll understand.'

His mind was reeling, but suddenly their pace increased and before long they were skimming across the ground at a fantastic pace and the landscape was a blur. He had no idea in which direction they were travelling or even how far they'd travelled, but then equally suddenly they slowed to a gentle pace once again. He looked around, but nothing was familiar. How he would ever find his way home again, he just didn't know... but did he want to go home again? It was then that he thought of his mum – she'd be desperate with worry; he felt he must get in touch with her; he didn't like the thought of her being sad. Could he phone her? After all, he had Jez's phone.

'Don't worry about your mum, Oliver, she's perfectly all right,' said the woman, as if reading his thoughts. 'She just wants you to concentrate all your energies on the quest before you – it's not just for your benefit that you have to find that house, it's for your mum's benefit too. Do it for her.'

A deep inner peace descended on him; he felt reassured, confident that his mum was all right, but why should that be? 'She doesn't know my mum, so how can she know how she's feeling, what she's thinking, even? How can Mum be "perfectly all right" with Jez around? Hey, perhaps she's kicked him out at last – well, good riddance if she has – good for you, Mum.' The thought brought a tremendous lightness to Oliver's spirit and he almost sang for joy.

The woman turned her face, that beautiful face, towards him and she nodded her head and smiled gently.

'Wow, there she goes again, she knows what I'm thinking. I'd better be very careful what I think while I'm with her.'

She gave him a sideways glance and smiled.

'Oh, er...' he said, aloud, and smiled back at her.

By this time, they had reached a small village and she turned in at the gate of one house that stood alone. It was a lovely house, bright and well kept – it looked very inviting. She opened the front door, which, it seemed, hadn't been locked, so Oliver wondered if maybe someone else lived here too.

'Who else lives here with you? Do you have a husband or a friend living with you?' he asked.

'No, I live alone, but I'm not here very often, only for special occasions or for special visitors like you.'

'So where do you normally live?'

'Oh, I have another extremely beautiful home in a fantastically beautiful place. You'd like it and I hope one day to meet you there. For now, though, we have to be practical; are you hungry?'

'Come to think of it, I believe I am – what time is it?' Oliver looked at his watch, but something had gone wrong with it, the fingers were simply whizzing round at a tremendous pace. 'Oh dear, my watch seems to have gone haywire, so I've no idea what time it's supposed to be.'

'So sorry,' she replied, 'I tend to forget that in my home things don't quite work as they do out in the world beyond. I live in a different time sphere, so that makes things such as your watch go a little crazy. It'll settle in a moment.'

Oliver didn't understand what she meant by a different time sphere, but although normally he tended to have a very questioning mind, for some reason what she'd said seemed to be totally unimportant, so he just let it slide and instead glanced at his watch again. 'Oh, it's working properly again, but is it really 7.30pm? Where has today gone? We were only out and about for a short time.'

'You'll find that time flies when you're with me, but just relax and enjoy your stay. Now, what would you like for your dinner? Do you want your favourite, sausage, beans and chips, and trifle to follow?'

'Oh, wow, how did you know those things were my favourites, are you a clairvoyant?'

'Oh no, very much the opposite: I know much about you because the Father gives me information as I need it – He is the only source of real knowledge and He will never deceive.'

'He sounds a fantastic person to know; I wish I had someone like Him in my life, to help me and tell me what's best.'

'One day you will, Oliver, one day all will become clear; trust me, I know it is going to happen, and on that day you will have great joy. For now, though – is it the sausage, beans and chips?'

'Can I really have those things?'

'Of course you can, unless you want something different. Perhaps you would like to try something you've never had before and have always wanted to try?'

'You are extremely kind, but no, I think I'll stick to what I know I like, except, perhaps… can I have an egg with it? I'm not allowed to have both egg and sausage at home.'

'That's fine. I'll just go and get it ready. As I don't have a television, perhaps you'd like to read a book or listen to music while I'm getting it? My music is different to anything you've heard before, so you may not like it.'

'Yes, I'd love to listen to your music. I like music and would love to learn to play an instrument; I like singing too, but at school they laugh at me and Jez won't let me sing at home – he says it's noisy screeching, like a cat in pain.'

'Well, if you want to sing here, please feel free to do so.' She went over to what he assumed was an MP3 player or similar, turned the music on and left the room. Oliver sank back in his chair and allowed the most wonderful music he'd ever heard to simply bathe him in its all-encompassing power. After a while, singers added a beautiful harmony. Their words were perfectly clear and were somewhat… *religious* was the only word he could come up with. He was completely absorbed in its beauty and, before he realised it, he was singing along with them. He had never heard the lyrics before, but he somehow knew them and was fluent in singing them out. His voice was totally in harmony with the other singers and his gentle voice drifted through to where the woman was. He didn't see how his voice was affecting the woman, but tears began to flow down her cheeks; only in her other home had she heard such a lovely voice – the joy that it brought her was immense.

Oliver knew that his experiences were changing him; something was stirring within him.

The track ended just as the woman brought the evening meal in on a lap tray.

'I thought we might eat informally tonight; are you happy to eat it off your knees?'

'No problem, it's what I'm used to at home – except that I rarely get a proper cooked meal, it's usually bread and jam, or sometimes just bread. Jez says it's a waste of good food, giving it to me. I really don't know why he hates me so much. I really liked him at first, but then he suddenly changed and he started to hit me and wouldn't allow my mum to show me any love. He said it would toughen me up and make a man of me. Anyway, thank you for this food and for your kindness, and you don't even know me.'

'But I do know you, Oliver, and yes, I do care about you. I want the very best for you and that is why I met with you today. Someone even greater than me sent me. He said to tell you, "All is going to change, be made new."'

'I don't think I understand what that means. How will all things change and be made new? Who's going to do what and when?'

'I can't really explain any more now, but I want you to trust me that what is planned is not going to harm you, but bless you. For now, be at peace and eat before it goes cold.'

He felt the peace flow over him and, although he'd had a million questions he'd wanted to ask, they no longer mattered, no longer seemed important. He took his first mouthful of the food and he was absolutely amazed, it was the most delightful taste ever. It looked exactly as sausage, egg, beans and chips would normally look, but the taste was out of this world. By the time he'd finished the trifle, he felt entirely satisfied. He needed nothing more; he had a lovely feeling of well-being. He had a glass of squash afterwards, and then they sat and chatted for quite some time. He felt so much at ease that he was able to share his heart with the woman and she simply listened, giving him her total attention. He offloaded a tremendous weight that evening and later felt the tremendous relief that it brought.

'Do you mind me asking, what is your name?' Oliver asked, having plucked up courage. 'I didn't like to ask you before.'

'I certainly don't mind you asking, I've been expecting you to ask me all along. My name is Marianne, the name chosen by the Father.'

'I like that name, I think it suits you, Oliver responded.

'Thank you,' Marianne replied.

'I almost forgot, I'm meant to be asking you, where's St Martin's Church?' Oliver suddenly remembered. 'Do you know, because I think I was told to ask you for directions? By the way, who sent you to meet me?'

'Well, it was the Father who sent me. He said you needed help and He also said you needed healing both in your body and your mind. As for St Martin's, yes, I know where it is and tomorrow I will help you to find it. Now I think you need to rest, you have a hectic day ahead of you tomorrow.'

'Before I sleep though, do I know the Father – how does He know me – can I meet Him?'

'You have many questions and you'll have many more in the days ahead. No, you don't know the Father, but one day you will meet Him and you will know Him. He knows you, though, and He loves you dearly.'

'How can He when we've never met? I don't understand.'

'I can't explain it now, it's not the right time, but please just trust me – everything that you are going to learn over the coming days is in your best interests and will help you one day to know and love the Father. Sleep now, Oliver, peace, be still.' She reached out her hand towards him and he immediately drifted off into a deep sleep. At which point, although he did not know it, Marianne picked him up as though he was a feather and took him upstairs and laid him on a bed.

That night Oliver slept more soundly than he had ever slept before; his mind was now at rest and he was entirely in a place of peace. This was not simply because he was free from conflict and fear, but because he had a sense of perfect well-being, of being cradled in love and care; exactly *whose* love and care he did not know, but it was something that felt very tangible. He did have a dream, but not one that evoked fear; rather, it was a message: 'Oliver, tomorrow you will meet a man at St Martin's Church and he will tell you what you must do next, where you must go and who you will meet next in your quest to find that house. Have no fear, but simply go and all will become clear.'

When he awoke he was at a loss to know where he was; it was not his own home. Then he remembered Marianne… Marianne's house? He quickly jumped out of bed and found that the room had an en suite, so he washed and cleaned his teeth… with his own toothbrush!

'This is weird,' he said in a whisper. 'What on earth is going on?' He returned to the bedroom to dress and was immediately amazed to find all his clothes clean and neatly laid out for him. Weird it might be, but this was amazing room service.

He went downstairs. He was not sure what to expect, but Marianne met him and welcomed him with a brief hug. How good that hug felt; he could not remember when he had last experienced real tenderness; it made him feel good about himself. Perhaps he did have some worth after all.

'Welcome, sleepy-head! Are you ready for some breakfast? What would you like? You can have anything at all,' Marianne told him, placing her arm across his shoulders.

'Anything at all?' he questioned.

'Yes, quite literally, so you just say what takes your fancy and I'll get it for you.'

'Wow, thanks! Can I have fruit juice, some cereal, and poached eggs on toast, or is that too much?'

'Not at all, what you've asked for comes well within the category of "anything", so choose your cereal from those on the table, and there's fruit juice there too, so please help yourself – and don't worry about whether you're having portions that are too big. Just feel free to have your fill. Oh, there's milk on the table too.'

Oliver went to the table and sat down in the place already laid out. He looked at the boxes of cereal, six in all, trying to decide which to have, but even as he watched, the array of cereals changed; they went through a cycle.

'Bizarre!' he chuckled. He waited for the frosted chocolate rice to come round again, grabbed it and poured what he felt he needed into his dish. He added milk and began to munch. It was truly delicious, more so than any cereal he had tasted before. He poured himself a mango juice and drank it down. He felt so good. Just as he finished his cereal, Marianne came in with his poached eggs on toast.

'Are you OK, Oliver? Are you ready for this or would you like more cereal?'

'I'm feeling great. No more cereal, thank you, but that looks wonderful – you are so kind to me. Are you not having breakfast too? I noticed you didn't eat dinner last night; do you have yours at a different time?'

'Yes, sort of. I have a special source of nourishment, but I do eat with my guests sometimes. Would you prefer it if I ate now?'

'Well, only if you want to or you're hungry. I like your company and want to be with you as much as possible. I've never had anyone spend time with just me before. I didn't realise how great it would be to have someone care the way you do. I feel loved.'

'I'm glad you feel that way, Oliver, because you are wonderfully made and you are greatly loved. Reject completely all the negative things that you've previously experienced and, in future, try hard not to take on board anything negative that people throw at you. You are special, you are lovely and you are destined for great things – plans that your Heavenly Father has for you, plans to help you flourish, and not to harm you, plans to give you future hope. You will achieve your deepest desire. Oliver, I have thoroughly enjoyed our time together. I am so privileged to have been the one chosen to meet with you, to care for you and to help you on your journey.'

Tears were rolling down Oliver's cheeks, tears that Marianne gently wiped away as she held him to her side. 'Never be ashamed to let tears flow,' she said. 'They help to dissolve pain and bring relief. I often weep with joy when I am in my Master's presence, and one day you will do the same. Now, if you have finished your breakfast, go and clean your teeth, we have to get going. Don't bother with all your belongings, they will follow you wherever you go.'

Oliver glanced at her quizzically, wondering how that could be, but her simple smile told him not to concern himself with the how and just to trust, so he went upstairs and cleaned his teeth. When he returned, he did have a question: 'Marianne, while I was sleeping last night, did you speak to me about going to St Martin's Church today?'

'Well, not exactly, yes you heard a voice, it was an inner voice preparing you for what lies ahead and what you can expect. You will experience that inner voice many times and always it will be for your good. Please remember what I said; have no fear about it, all will be well; be at peace.'

Whenever Marianne spoke those words to him, Oliver immediately sensed a feeling of perfect well-being flowing through him from head to foot. What was it about her that was so calming? He just didn't understand, but it was a wonderful experience. 'Are you coming with me to St Martin's, Marianne?'

'I will take you there, but I can't come in with you. You will be well looked after, but another has the instructions for the next stage of your quest. Now, if you are ready, we need to get started; it is quite a way.'

'Don't you have a car to take you places?' he asked.

'No, I don't need a car. When I walk the world passes quickly by and I'm soon at my destination, as you will find today.'

With that, they left the house and Oliver noticed that she didn't lock the door. She took his hand and they began to walk; after a few short steps he glanced back, but the house was not there any more, only a green meadow remained in its place. He frowned, but before he could say anything, they were once again skimming along at a tremendous speed and the landscape around them was just a blur. He had no inkling of direction, nor of the places they were passing; Marianne didn't speak and he wasn't sure he could, even if he'd tried. The thoughts of what lay ahead filled his mind and, although he knew the eventual destination – that house – he didn't know why he couldn't simply travel straight to it. Even as that thought passed through his mind, he heard the voice of Marianne speaking to him, in his thoughts: 'It is simply because you have many lessons to learn beforehand. All of these lessons will prepare you for what you will experience after entering that house for real.'

'I wonder… can I communicate with her in the same manner?' He tried it. 'Marianne, when will I eventually get to that house?' he asked, in his mind.

'That, I'm afraid, I can't tell you. Be patient, it will happen, but only at just the right moment when all things planned for you are completed.' She glanced at him and smiled her beautiful smile that was so reassuring and comforting. How could a smile be so powerful and say so much? He gripped Marianne's hand even tighter; she really was a lovely person and he would be so sad to part from her when they got to St Martin's Church.

It would seem that moment was now near; their pace began to slow and soon they were at walking pace again.

Then Oliver noticed a church building before them, a large building with a steeple. There was a graveyard around it, and there was an arched gateway. They walked up to the gate and Marianne spoke: 'This is it, Oliver, this is where we must go our separate ways, but you are stronger now and you will handle it well – be confident and step out like the young man that you're becoming. Before you go, though...' She reached out and drew Oliver close and at the same time, he threw his arms around her.

'Thank you,' he whispered.

'You are very welcome; it has been a great pleasure for me. Goodbye.' She gave him another of her beautiful smiles and suddenly he felt three metres tall. He turned towards the gate, but then took one final glance back – Marianne had gone.

3. Joshua

Oliver began what seemed to him the longest walk of his life, though in reality it was only a few metres. He approached the heavy entrance door and turned the handle; it made a loud click as the latch lifted, but the door swung open easily and noiselessly. It looked like a traditional church inside, with wooden pews and stained-glass windows, but there was no smell of age; instead it smelt fresh and clean – it felt inviting and welcoming. Initially Oliver thought that no one was in there, but then he noticed someone sitting in the shadows on the far side from the door. Oliver walked slowly in that direction, his footsteps gently echoing in the empty building. There was no movement from the man and Oliver began to wonder if he was asleep.

As he got closer, Oliver spoke: 'Hello, sorry to disturb you. I'm Oliver Carrick and I'm looking for someone – I mean, I'm meant to be meeting someone. Can you help me?'

The man seemed suddenly aware of his presence and got to his feet, though in reality he was not much taller standing than he'd been while sitting. Oliver could see that he was a little old man with grey hair and a very happy-looking face; he wore a dark green, well-pressed suit and he had brown, highly polished shoes.

'Oliver! Delighted to meet you, Oliver!' he said, extending his hand and warmly shaking Oliver's. 'I've been expecting you, but I'm afraid I was completely lost in thought. I was miles away. Anyway, you're here and I am pleased to say that I've been designated as your host for the next twenty-four hours, so I hope you'll be happy staying with me as I explain the next steps in your quest to find that house.'

'How come everyone knows me, and knows all about the house in my dream? Do you know Marianne, by any chance – did she tell you about me?'

'Oh, yes, I know Marianne very well, we've known each other for... well, forever. No, she didn't tell me. The message and instructions came from the Master.'

'The Master!' exclaimed Oliver incredulously. 'Who is the Master?

'He is the One we serve – He is the Heavenly Father to all who believe.'

'So He's sort of your Father and Marianne's Father too – are you related?'

The old man chuckled, exactly the kind of chuckle that Marianne had. 'I really can't explain it now, but we do indeed have the same Master and He is very much alive, though some call Him "The Ancient of Days". One day, after you've visited that house, you will find that so many things click into place. Be patient, all will become clear and one day you too will know Him for yourself. Marianne and I are sort of brother and sister – though not in the way you're probably thinking. Trust me, one day you will understand, so for now be at peace.'

Once again, those words touched a spot in Oliver's heart and that lovely feeling of warmth and well-being poured through the whole of his body. His uncertainties no longer mattered and questions could wait.

'Please will you come with me now? My house is not too far away and there you will be fed and find rest for the night, for you must embark on a difficult journey tomorrow, so you need to be fully prepared both physically and emotionally.' He placed his arm around Oliver's shoulders; they stepped outside and set off walking along the road. They had not travelled far when, just like before, their pace increased and the landscape once again became a blur. It never ceased to amaze Oliver.

'Wow, this is incredible; travelling with your sister was just like this,' the thought went through his mind.

Then, as with Marianne, that inaudible yet nevertheless clear reply came from the old man: 'You have cars, buses and planes, but where I come from we don't have such transport. We always travel this way and it's actually quicker, as we don't experience traffic jams and accidents! Don't you think that's better?'

'It's fantastic. I wish it was always like this for us, but what about when it comes to crossing the sea – what happens then?'

'Just the same; we walk everywhere, whether it's on land or on water – it's quite useful,' the old man chuckled again. Then he gave Oliver a sideways glance and a smile – oh, that smile was just as potent as Marianne's had been and that inner peace flowed over him. He knew he was in safe hands.

Eventually, the pace slowed and soon they were walking normally, towards a house; was it the same house that he'd visited with Marianne? It looked remarkably similar, but the setting was very different – all these experiences were very confusing. They approached the front door and, once again, it was unlocked.

'These people seem very trusting when it comes to home security, but maybe he has a wife,' Oliver thought.

The man chuckled and spoke aloud: 'Our houses have special protection, so we don't need locks. Guards are posted all around; today you can't see them, but one day you will. No, Oliver, I don't have a wife, I'm not married. Where I come from we're all looked after superbly and lack nothing, but I always have my assigned tasks. While I'm here I do have to do things that I don't normally have to do: for instance, I'll be preparing your food – I think you'll enjoy it, though.'

They entered the house and Oliver was immediately aware that everything was much the same as it had been in Marianne's; it looked the same, smelled the same and had the same sense of peace and well-being. He immediately felt at home and relaxed. He glanced at his watch and it was at it again, the hands were whizzing around at an enormous pace.

'Oh!' he gasped. 'My watch has gone haywire again.'

'Sorry, Oliver,' the man responded. 'We always tend to forget about that sort of thing when we're in your time sphere. There, has that fixed it?'

'Yes! But you didn't do anything, so how did you fix it?'

'Well, I did do something, though to you it would have been imperceptible.'

'So why is the time-... sphere, did you call it, different in yours and Marianne's houses?'

'Hmm, that's difficult to explain; all I can say is, where we come from we calculate time rather differently. Here, time is very important and generally determines most things, but where I come from time is unimportant, of no consequence, we just do what needs doing as and when required – it is fantastically freeing; we're not constantly looking at our watches and clocks. If you look around you here, I have no timepiece of any description. While we're here we simply have to be aware of other people's needs. So what time do you say it is now?'

'Gosh, it's six o'clock. We didn't seem to be walking for long, so how come the time has passed so quickly? Did you somehow speed it up? Eh, by the way, what do I call you?'

'You can call me Joshua. No, I didn't speed up the time, but while we're travelling, you are completely unaware of time passing. Well, as it's six o'clock, you are probably ready for your dinner, especially as you missed lunch. What would you like? You can choose absolutely anything you fancy. So what will it be?'

'Joshua, you are very kind, but I can't put you to a lot of trouble. Actually, I'd really like some Chinese food – chicken chow mein, but I'd be happy with anything – fish and chips or even something on toast.'

'Chinese is absolutely fine and no trouble whatsoever,' he smiled. 'I thought you might choose that. What would you like to drink – I'm guessing it will be mango and pineapple juice?'

'Oh, wow, yes please, Joshua, that would be great. You seem to have everything available – my favourite food and drink! How lucky am I?! You're spoiling me – Jez would never allow me to have such a fantastic meal... I don't know what's going to happen when I go home.'

'Be at peace about that, Oliver. I think you will find that things are very different when you go back to your home. In the meantime, I'll put some quiet music on while I go and prepare your meal. So, sit back, make yourself comfortable and let peace flow over you – let all anxiety lift from you. I won't be many moments.'

Oliver lay back in his chair; it seemed like the very chair he'd sat in while with Marianne. The music was nothing like anything he'd heard before and nothing like anything they'd play on the radio – 'but they ought to,' he thought. It was so very soothing and as he listened, he felt he could easily have drifted off into a deep sleep. Suddenly, though, the gorgeous smell of his Chinese meal wafted over him and at that precise moment Joshua walked in carrying a big tray with a variety of dishes on it, and these he offloaded onto the table.

'OK, Oliver, please come to the table if you're ready and help yourself – it's all for you, so please don't be afraid to take as much as you want. I don't know whether you ever give thanks for your food, but may I do so before you eat?'

Oliver nodded; what he was supposed to do he wasn't sure, so he simply bowed his head and listened. Oliver didn't really know what being 'blessed' meant: Joshua spoke some lovely words of thanks to his God – clearly someone he knew intimately, loved dearly and whom he knew would be listening, although He was unseen. He thanked his God for what had been provided, asked that Oliver would be greatly *blessed* in eating it, and concluded with an 'Amen'. Well, if blessing meant he would enjoy the food and feel good afterwards, it certainly worked. The food was sumptuous and what Joshua had provided was far more than he needed.

'Joshua, that was fantastic, you are a great cook. Thank you so much.'

'Now, then, I should have asked when you requested your first course, what would you like to follow? I think I can guess, but you tell me.'

'Actually that's a simple choice to make; again – waffles with maple syrup and vanilla ice cream, please?'

'But of course you can, it's exactly what I would have chosen for you. I won't be a moment.' He walked off to the kitchen and Oliver noticed how sprightly he was. He didn't know how old he was, of course, but he guessed he might be about eighty. He was extremely agile, whatever his age. Joshua returned very quickly and placed Oliver's dessert before him.

Oliver's face beamed at the fantastic feast he was having. 'I just can't believe this,' he said. 'I've never before in my life had such a feast. Mum will never believe it when I tell her.'

The meal over, Joshua cleared the table and Oliver was invited to return to the armchair. Then, Joshua sat in one opposite.

'Is there anything you want to ask me, Oliver? If I can help, I will, but there are some things I'm not allowed to tell you. Anyway, try me and we'll see.'

Oliver thought for a few moments before saying anything, but then he said, 'What's this all about? Why am I having to go on this strange adventure? What is going to happen next – tomorrow, for instance? Can you tell me these things?'

'I can answer some of them, but what the next stage is going to be will be revealed in full later. I can tell you that some things will greatly test you, but you must be strong, brave and very determined – it will all be worth it in the end. You know, of course, that your purpose is to find that house of your dreams. When you do find it, the quest will be complete and many things will become new. Why do you have to go through this strange adventure? Because there is much for you to learn, and especially you need to learn how to trust your Heavenly Father. I sense a question rising in your mind about that, but getting to meet, to know, to love and trust Him is the essence of all things working harmoniously together for your good and your family's good. One day you will experience something that you have always longed for but which has always seemed to be an impossibility.'

'But how can I get to know the Father – I don't even know where He is, so I don't know where to look for Him.'

'Oliver, you will find the Father when you seek Him with all your heart; when you want to know Him and are ready to surrender your will to His.'

'Hmm, when you and Marianne speak of the Father, are you referring to some sort of god? Is that what you mean?'

'Got it in one! Well done, Oliver, but he's not just "some sort of god". He's the true and living God. You've taken a very significant step there, but don't rush, just let simple truths come to you little by little – as indeed they will, but the final steps will be taken in that house.'

'So, Joshua, are you saying that your God is real? How do you know? Jez always says that God's not real, He's just some imaginary crutch that weak people invent.'

'Hmm, quite a common phrase, but entirely wrong. I know God exists because I meet with Him and converse with Him every day – He sends me out on assignments, such as meeting with you and helping you in your quest. Sadly, many people don't want to know him, so even refuse to find out the truth for themselves. Also there is one who hates the Father and does his best to prevent people from seeking Him and finding Him, but I urge you not to let anything or anyone put you off; entering into a relationship with the Father, it is something you will never regret.'

'Thanks, that sort of makes sense – you must enjoy having such a close relationship with Him, but doesn't He frighten you sometimes?'

Joshua laughed as he responded. 'Our relationship is the best imaginable. Does he frighten me sometimes? Not frighten, but I do hold Him in complete awe; none of us must ever take Him for granted or show any contempt – after all, He is God, Almighty God, King of kings and Lord of lords. There is no one greater.'

'I need to think about this. My family's never been religious.'

'But you've been to Sunday school, haven't you?'

Oliver was surprised. 'Well – I sort of remember that, now you mention it. How did you know? I think Mum took me to church a few times, when she didn't have a boyfriend... It was ages ago. Anyway, I... er... I don't know what's true and what's just imagination. You and

Marianne are the first people I've ever met who seem to have a definite relationship with God. Good for you! But I don't think I could ever feel like you do.'

'Be at peace, Oliver; I don't want you to feel stressed, no one is rushing you into anything. Faith is something that comes when something special happens inside you – in that moment you just know. For now, just relax and enjoy your stay.'

For the rest of the evening they sat and chatted easily. Joshua was easy to talk to, so Oliver opened his heart to him – sharing the important experiences of his life to date. His greatest longing was, and had been for many years, he said, for his real family to be back together, and how he hated his mum having all her different boyfriends. He went on to say how he knew she was trying to fill an empty void in her life where his dad should have been, but it didn't work, she was still desperately depressed most of the time. Jez's presence only made matters worse and prevented Oliver from being close to and receiving love from his mum. Jez, he added, said showing Oliver love was 'childish and he needed to grow up' so he wouldn't let Oliver near his mother or her near him. He also explained how, when he had nightmares and woke up screaming, it was Jez who came in and demanded that he just stop making such a racket and how if he didn't he would give him a hard slap, something his mum hated, but she was too frightened to do anything about.

'Your predicament, your sadness, your loneliness and your desperation has reached the ears, the eyes and the heart of the Father and change is coming – all will be made new and you will rejoice again. Do you want this?'

'Oh, more than anything – it would be absolutely fantastic, but I can't believe it can ever be different – Jez will never allow it to happen if he's still around.'

'Have no concerns about Jez, he is a spent force. So, Oliver, how much do you want what the Father wants for you – what are you prepared to do to see it become reality?'

'I think I'd do almost anything – especially if it meant Mum and Dad were back together again. It's what I really, *really* want. But can that ever happen? If it can, yes, I'm up for whatever it takes.'

'Your sincerity will be put to the test in pursuit of your quest, and I can tell you that it will demand total devotion and grim determination; it won't be easy, but you must persevere if you want to attain the Father's best. Remember this; listen carefully when that inner voice issues words of encouragement.'

A frown crossed Oliver's face. 'I'm not sure what you mean; what do I have to do to find that house? Can't you just take me there? I thought Marianne was going to and then I thought it was going to be you, but now you seem to be saying that no one's going to take me: so how do I find it?'

'Be at peace, Oliver. You're right, no one is going to take you, but help will be at hand. Just believe and trust and all will become clear. Remember, no one is expecting you to do anything that's impossible, but sometimes it's through difficulties that we achieve the most. Remember this: it is through tremendous pressure that diamonds are formed; it is because of irritations that pearls are formed, and gold must be subjected to great heat in order to become pure.'

'I'll try to remember your words, but I don't really understand what you're saying to me. Anyway, I said I would do almost anything and I'll always do my best.'

By the time they'd finished talking it was bedtime, and Oliver was more than ready. He felt tired and mentally exhausted; so all he wanted to do was tumble into bed and sleep. They said their goodnights and Oliver went upstairs. All his things, both in the bedroom and bathroom, were exactly as he had left them at the start of the day. It was uncanny – although the house was in a different location, it was, nonetheless, the same house. He climbed into bed, and though he began to think about the events of the day and all that Joshua had shared, tiredness overwhelmed him and he was fast asleep after a few minutes.

He woke up a few hours into the night and the house was silent, so he could not understand what had woken him. He turned over and quickly fell asleep again. It was during this part of the night that he began to dream and, as usual, he found himself walking towards that house. This time he stood still for quite some time and simply looked at it, as if willing something or someone to appear, but to all intents and purposes, the house was deserted – there was no sign of life anywhere. For the first time ever he realised something – the house stood entirely alone, simply surrounded by grass; it had no garden, so no flowers, and there were no bushes or trees anywhere near. Did this house really exist, or was it just going to disappear at any moment? He didn't stay any longer, but began to move on, and eventually he came to a bench and sat down. As he glanced around there was no one to be seen anywhere in any direction, but then suddenly he was aware that someone had sat down on the bench alongside him. Oliver tried hard not to stare at the woman, but could not resist sideways glances.

'Hello, Oliver, I thought I might find you here. Do you mind if I talk to you?'

'OK, but who are you and why did you expect to meet me here?'

'Oh, I'm simply a friend and I've been sent here to give you a message. Tomorrow you are to go to the local marketplace and sit on the red seat and the first person who comes and sits beside of you is going to care for you for the next twenty-four hours. He may not seem like anyone you've met before, but trust him and go with him.'

Oliver felt a little uneasy; it had been drummed into them at school that they must never go off with strangers, no matter how kind they appeared. However, this was somehow all part of his recurring dream – unreal, yet with a genuine element such as he'd found with Marianne and Joshua. Before Oliver could say anything more or ask any more questions, the woman had gone as quickly as she'd appeared. Again Oliver looked all around, but there was no one to be seen anywhere. It was seemingly soon afterwards that he awoke and found it was almost eight o'clock. He jumped out of bed and went to the bathroom, where he showered to wash away the sleepiness of the night, brushed his hair and returned to the bedroom to dress. As he dressed, he remembered the dream and today's instructions – or was it merely a dream? Perhaps Joshua would know. Downstairs there was a wonderful smell of breakfast cooking.

'Good morning and welcome, Oliver. Are you ready for breakfast?'

'Yes please, Joshua, the smell of cooking is making me feel very hungry.'

'What would you like this morning? You can have anything you fancy and there's cereal and fruit juice on the table.'

'I actually fancy what I can smell – is it eggs and bacon?'

'It is, and there's sausage, hash browns, fried bread, baked beans and fresh tomatoes – could you eat some of all, and would you like toast too?'

'Wow, yes, everything please – I've never had food like this before! It's going to be hard going home; there I'm lucky if I get bread and jam, it's usually just bread and water. Do you always prepare such feasts?'

'I only prepare such food when I have an assignment such as I have with you; normally, where I come from, the Master organises the banquets and teams of great chefs prepare everything to order. The food we have each day is different – the choices are truly amazing. The Master only provides the very best at His banquets. Anyway, I think you have something you want to share with me and ask my opinion about – am I right?'

'Do I? Oh yes, I'd forgotten my dream. I dreamed that I met a woman who told me that today I have to go to the marketplace and sit on a red seat and there I'll meet a man I won't immediately take to. Was it just a dream, or do I really have to go to the marketplace, as the woman said? Do you know what town it will be?'

'Obviously it was a dream, but not just a dream; yes, you are to go as directed, and yes, I know which town and will take you there. What you will hear from this person is extremely important, so listen carefully, step out confidently, persevere diligently and arrive safely. This will be your third and final encounter with a guide. I urge you to stay focused and don't be tempted to give up. So, now, help yourself to cereal and fruit juice and I will get your cooked breakfast ready for when you are.'

Oliver looked at the six cereal options on the table and, as before, the six options changed – this was certainly a bizarre house, full of surprises. He selected one and some fruit juice and just as he finished Joshua entered with his cooked food. It was a most delicious breakfast and Oliver quickly polished off the whole lot. Joshua cleared everything away and announced that they would have to go very soon, so Oliver went upstairs to clean his teeth and make final preparations for the journey. When he came down again, Joshua was waiting and they left the house together. Joshua took Oliver's hand and they began to walk. Oliver glanced back over his shoulder and realised that the house had disappeared. Now their pace increased and soon the landscape around them once again became a blur.

'I wonder how far it is to the town marketplace,' he wondered, forgetting that Joshua would know his thoughts.

'It's not far in my terms,' Joshua announced, 'but in yours it would be a long way. But time flashes by here, so it will not seem to be very long.'

'What town is it?' Oliver enquired. 'Is it one I'll recognise?'

'No, you won't recognise it, you've never been there before. I can't tell you its name, but it wouldn't mean anything to you if I did. Anyway, we are almost there, so do you remember what you have got to do and who you're going to meet, or at least, what was said about this person?'

'Yes, I remember, but I don't know why I might not immediately take to him – unless it's Jez, of course; I certainly wouldn't feel comfortable with him and I'd probably run a mile.'

Oliver glanced across at the old man and he was smiling back at him. 'No, it's certainly not Jez; indeed, this person couldn't look less like him. Remember, Oliver, don't let first impressions colour your attitude or reaction. Let the person speak for themselves – not just their words, but their attitude towards you and their care for you. Let love swell your heart.'

Again a frown spread across Oliver's face, but before he could think anything more, the pace rapidly decreased and very soon they were walking normally again. They were in a bustling town, with people coming and going in all directions. Joshua was right, this town was entirely unfamiliar; Oliver had never visited it before. He tried to look into the shop windows as he passed, but realised that for some reason he couldn't see in, not even to determine what sort of shops they were. It was all very strange indeed. They soon came to the market square, and there were many coloured seats dotted around; people occupied most of the seats, but he could see that the red seat was vacant.

'I have to leave you now, Oliver,' Joshua announced, 'but please go to the allotted seat and you won't be alone for long.' He took Oliver's hand and gently shook it. 'Thank you for the time you've spent with me, you have been a delightful guest and I wish you great peace and blessing in all your journeying, and encourage you to listen carefully to that small voice within – you will never be alone, no matter what you may feel.'

'Thank you, Joshua, I'm going to miss you; you have been so kind to me and I will never forget you. I hope we will meet again sometime.'

4. Gabriel

Oliver turned his head, a tear in his eye, and when he turned back again, Joshua was nowhere to be seen. Had he simply melted into the bustling crowd? Oliver didn't think he'd had time to do that. Joshua was just like his house – there one second, but gone the next. What was it about these people? He walked over towards the red seat, fully expecting someone else to get there before him, but no one did. He sat and looked around, wondering if he could distinguish among the crowd the person designated to be his next host, but no one looked at all likely. Perhaps Joshua's estimation had been a bit out, maybe the person had been delayed somewhere. He sat and 'people watched' as he waited and noticed among the largely well-dressed passers-by an old tramp-like figure shuffling along, but then as he watched him he saw him turn and walk towards the seat where Oliver was.

'Oh no,' he thought to himself. 'He can't sit here, I'm waiting for someone.'

Nevertheless, sit there the tramp did, and Oliver wondered if he should say anything. He glanced sideways at the man. He was quite old, he had a big bushy beard and his hair was long and unkempt – or at least what Oliver could see of it, poking from under the man's grubby checked cap. His clothes had long since seen better days –

baggy trousers turned up at the bottom, a worn-out tweedy jacket, and boots that barely covered his feet due to the number of holes in the uppers. In some places, the holes in his boots coincided with the holes in his socks. As Oliver looked at the man, he turned his head, and Oliver noticed his beautiful, kindly blue eyes. His face creased into a smile as he spoke.

'Hello, I believe you're Oliver Carrick, but I'm not quite what you were expecting, I guess, but I am the person designated to host you for the next twenty-four hours and then to help you on your way. I hope you're not too disappointed or shocked by my looks, because really I'm just an ordinary person who simply looks different, dresses differently and lives differently.'

'Oh... er... er,' Oliver stuttered, 'sorry, I guess you knew what I was thinking, but honestly it was only because I didn't think you could possibly be the person I was supposed to meet; I mean, you look so different from Marianne and Joshua. Please forgive me if I offended you.'

'No offence taken, I am quite used to people's reactions; some can be very offensive, even rude and hostile. No, yours was a perfectly natural reaction. You had no real warning as to what to expect, except, I think, that I would be different. So here I am, this is me, Gabriel.' As he said this, he reached out and gently shook Oliver's hand, and a slight tingle, like a very mild electric shock, passed through Oliver's hand and arm and down his body. It made Oliver jump slightly.

'Sorry, Oliver,' he said with a smile. 'Only sensitive people ever feel that, and I believe you are a sensitive person with a gentle spirit. I rather fear you are bullied by your peers, is that correct?'

'Yes, you're right, but it's not just by kids at school. It's at home too – Mum's boyfriends are less than kind to me – they hate me and resent my being there. I have no real time alone with Mum and it hurts.'

Gabriel reached out his hand and squeezed Oliver's shoulder. As their eyes met, both had tears running down their cheeks.

'Don't worry, Oliver, things are going to change, and one day you'll be happier than you've ever been before. It's for that reason that you're going through all that you're experiencing at present and why the quest to find that house is necessary. At times, it will be tough going, but don't doubt the goal and don't be tempted to give up. Remember what you said to Joshua, you are willing to do almost anything to achieve that goal. I want to encourage you further – accept and face up to whatever challenge is thrown at you, it will be worth it.'

'I really will do my best, but facing up to difficulties is not something I'm good at. I'm not physically strong and neither am I mentally strong – I've learned to run away when trouble comes my way, except that I have sometimes been violent with teachers when they refused to listen to my side of things. But that's not the real me.'

'Ah, I'm not sure about that; I think that anger is part of you. Allowing it to control your reactions is not good, but if it's controlled and used to feed your resolve, then it can be very powerful and help you succeed. Anger is a natural reaction, but it has to be channelled.'

'Can you help me, Gabriel?'

'That's partly what I'm here for. However, for now we have to get going, it's not very far but we have things to talk through and I don't feel it's appropriate to do it here; also, you'll need to eat and food awaits at my home.'

At that, they rose to their feet and began to walk together. Progress was painfully slow as Gabriel took his shuffling steps, but after a few moments he reached out and took Oliver's hand, and immediately their surroundings became a blur. This was still not something Oliver could get his head round; it was what always seemed to happen, but it was still a very strange experience. The more he thought about it, everything about these encounters and the journeying was very strange; why was he doing all of this? Oh yes, he knew what the ultimate purpose was, but why did he have to face everything that he was going through, and why was he being told that many difficulties lay ahead? Why couldn't one of his guides simply bypass the challenges ahead and take him to that house?

And that was another thing, what was so special about that house – he'd only seen it in a dream, so did it really exist and if it did, what difference would finding it make? Too many things didn't make sense to him and nobody was giving him any definitive explanation. Surely if they all knew what his destination was, and clearly, they did know, then why wouldn't they explain what it was about that house that made it so imperative that he visit it? Everyone seemed to be of the same opinion – visiting that house would be a good thing and lead to greater things. Could they be wrong? His dreams about the house had always resulted in something or somebody unpleasant chasing him, so why wouldn't a visit in the flesh produce exactly the same frightening outcome?

Suddenly the pace slowed and soon they were back to the same shuffling steps. Oliver looked all around and his heart sank. The lively bustle of the town centre had given way to a totally rundown area where the buildings were derelict and many were boarded up. They were now walking towards one of the dilapidated properties and Oliver feared the worst.

'Oh no, surely not,' he thought. 'We can't possibly be staying here – I bet it's rat-infested. No one could live here.'

'Sorry,' said Gabriel, 'but this is home for now; it may not look like the Ritz, but it's got a roof to keep any rain out. It really isn't too bad when you get used to it, and you'll only be here for one night – actually, you might be surprised by your experience here.'

They entered the derelict building, and the inside entirely matched what Oliver had seen on the outside. This was not a habitable home, it didn't have any home comforts, it didn't have chairs or a table, rubble littered the floor and everything was thick with dust. How could anyone possibly live in a place like this? Did Gabriel really consider this to be home? Was he going to have to stay here in these terrible conditions, and where was he going to sleep, surely not among all this muck and rubbish?

Gabriel's reaction clearly indicated that he knew exactly what Oliver was thinking and how uncomfortable he was in such a hovel and in such conditions. 'Be at peace, Oliver, all will become clear and after lunch you will see and experience yet more – all of this is a preparation for what lies ahead. Before that, though, you need to eat, so make the most of what's available here. There are cardboard boxes in the corner over there. Bring a couple for us to sit on. In the meantime, I'll go and prepare food for you.'

Gabriel went out through a doorway into another part of the house; maybe it was a kitchen area, but what sort of kitchen could there be in a dump like this? Oliver grabbed two cardboard boxes and flattened them on the floor in the centre of the room, where he sat down cross-legged and waited for Gabriel to return. Moments later Gabriel came back carrying an enamel plate with a doorstop of a sandwich on it and an old jam-jar filled with water. He passed these to Oliver and Oliver looked at them, wondering how appetising they would be. What sort of food preparation would there be in a dilapidated building like this? The point was, though, Oliver was hungry and so he put aside his natural reservations.

'Thank you, Gabriel,' he responded. He hesitatingly took a bite and his eyes lit up. It was a cheese sandwich, but it was far superior to any cheese sandwich he had ever tasted before. It looked very normal, but tasted anything but normal. He took a swig of the water and that also was extremely pleasant; sweet, pure water with no aftertaste whatsoever. How could someone who lived in such terrible conditions provide such perfect food?

'I can only offer fruit now, Oliver; I have an apple, an orange and a banana – which would you like?'

'Please could I have the banana? That sandwich was very filling, but a banana would just finish lunch perfectly. How on earth can you provide such lovely food?'

'Of course you can. You know, people can sometimes be very kind, so don't be tempted to think the worst of people;

I believe that showing respect and kindness towards others often elicits respect and kindness in return. Sadly, however, it's not always the case, but if people are unkind, don't retaliate, simply dismiss it from your mind and move on. Taking such things to heart only really affects you, making you extremely miserable, and that can lead to irrational behaviour. Often it's because a person responds to others' unkind treatment that they are encouraged to do it even more. Refuse to react and often they quickly give up trying to hurt or provoke. I know it's hard to suppress reactions, but it does often work, I can vouch for that. I'm sure you can imagine what sort of comments and treatment I attract.'

Oliver nodded his head; all that Gabriel was saying resonated with him. He now realised that the bullying had caused him to lash out and the teachers had been in the line of fire. Gabriel was right, dismissing the taunts and refusing to rise to the bait was by far the best option: this was something he would do his best to put into practice in future. Now, lunch being over, Gabriel explained what the afternoon activities would be.

'No doubt you see me as a down and out – a tramp, but actually I'm not. My assignment, just for a brief season until someone else can be appointed, is to care for people who are homeless and look very much like I do now. I go out and spend time with them and they see me as one of them, and that enables me to get close to them and minister to their needs; if I wasn't dressed like this, I wouldn't be able to get anywhere near them and certainly wouldn't be allowed into their circle. They're very suspicious of anyone who looks well dressed – in fact they will be highly suspicious of you, but the fact that you're with me will, I hope, put them at their ease. Are you ready and willing to come with me? I think you will glean much from meeting them.'

'Well, yes, I suppose so, but I don't want to cause any problems for you – I don't want them to reject you because of me.'

'Don't let that worry you, just be relaxed and if they ask, just tell them the truth, you're going through a difficult patch at present and we met and you have accepted my help and you're even bedding down for the night at my shelter. I think they'll be happy at that.'

Oliver still felt a little dubious, but concluded that Gabriel would know these people best and would be alongside him throughout the experience, or at least he hoped he would, as he didn't feel confident to face the situation alone. He'd never been good with strangers and a number of people who looked similar to Gabriel was something of a frightening prospect, especially if they were in the least suspicious of him or even hostile towards him. There was one big consolation, at least he didn't have anything that was worth mugging him for – except perhaps his watch and, of course, he still had Jez's phone.

'Ah, the phone,' he thought. 'It's strange that it hasn't rung all the time I've been away. Jez is always getting phone calls; perhaps the battery's flat.' He checked the charge level and it was still full, but now, just in case, he switched it off – 'Best if it doesn't ring while I'm out and about with Gabriel.'

Gabriel looked at him and nodded; he knew what had been passing through his mind.

'OK,' he said, 'let's get going; I normally make contact with them either early each morning or afternoon.'

'What do you do with them?' Oliver asked, as they began to walk together.

'Oh, anything they need – maybe just talk with them, or perhaps wash their feet. Many of them get very sore feet from pounding the streets and, needless to say, their feet get very sweaty or even wet and sometimes the skin begins to go a little rotten, so they do smell rather. Therefore, I wash and dress their wounds and give them fresh clean socks or even shoes. There is a church nearby that provides donated clothes, so I obtain what they need from there; often they're too proud to do it for themselves. The church also provides an evening meal, so I have to persuade them to go and get a good meal inside them. After that, they sleep rough – in doorways or alleyways, or some opt for a derelict building such as mine. Some sleep on benches at the coach or train station, but often the police or some other official move them on. I also give them a little money, only just enough for a cup of tea; some save it up for cigarettes – but it's worse if it goes on alcohol or drugs. If I suspect anyone is doing drugs I stop giving them money.'

'But where do you get money from – you seem to be extremely poor yourself?'

'As I said, I'm not exactly what I seem and I do have access to a limited amount of money that's been provided for my care of these very needy people.' Suddenly their pace increased and once again the landscape flashed by. Only moments later, it seemed, they slowed and Oliver could see that they were in a slum area of the town or city (he didn't know which). Initially it seemed to be entirely deserted, but then he caught glimpses of one or two shuffling figures and the sound of an angry voice coming from one particular building, which Oliver soon found out was being used as a squat.

'Oh dear, it sounds as though someone has upset James again. He has a rather a short fuse and easily gets upset. I wonder what it's all about this time. Now, then, James,' Gabriel said in a calming voice, 'what is all the fuss about? Take a breather, I'm sure we can sort it out.'

'Huh,' the man called James grunted, 'it's all right for you, but this old soak has stolen my fags and he doesn't even smoke.'

'It's a lie,' growled the other man. 'I ain't touched his fags; try the lining of his coat, that's where most things end up. Be careful if yer shoves yer hand in, though, he's probably got mice livin' in there as well.'

'Now, then, Albert,' said Gabriel with a grin, 'don't be cheeky to your elders.'

'Who're you calling old?' James protested. 'I bet you're older than me. Anyway, what's that lad doing with you? Just here to snoop, I bet. Come here, boy.'

Oliver took a couple of steps towards the man, but not within arm's length, in case he suddenly lashed out. That's something he'd learned in his dealings with Jez, though Jez was much younger and fitter than this man James looked.

'What are you doing here? We're not a sideshow at the fair! I bet you're just a nosy brat, come to make fun of us.'

Oliver started to respond. 'No, that's not true...' but Gabriel came to his rescue.

'James, just leave the lad alone, he's not much better off than you. He's experiencing a bad time and I've taken him under my wing; he'll only be with me for a day and then he has a long and difficult journey ahead of him. Anyway, are your feet troubling you again? Is that what's making you so tetchy?'

'They're killing me,' James responded with a grimace on his face, 'but my fags have gone and you know what I'm like without my fags.'

'Don't I and everyone else know only too well? Sit down and take your boots and socks off and I'll get some water.' Gabriel disappeared into the bowels of the property and came back moments later with an enamel bowl of water, a towel, soap and some sort of cream. He knelt down at James' bare feet – feet that looked very sore and the stench of which filled the air.

'How on earth can Gabriel be so near and seemingly oblivious to the smell?' thought Oliver.

Gabriel's reply came straight back to him, silently, inside his head: 'Partly because I'm used to it, but also because this man doesn't need my aversion, he gets that all too readily from others. He's very aware of the terrible stench, but the change you'll see in him when I've finished will tell its own story.'

James drew a deep breath as he immersed each foot in the water that contained some sort of antiseptic. Gabriel gently massaged the tender skin, washed his feet with the soap, and then James withdrew them one by one. Now the towel came into use; his feet were dried and the ointment applied. Oliver looked closely and noticed a transformation; the skin looked pink and normal with no sign of the soreness. Gabriel now produced a pair of clean socks and James pulled them on. As he did so, Gabriel sprinkled talc into James' boots and James pulled them on too. With that, both men stood up and James threw his arms around Gabriel. 'Thank you so much, you're a good man.'

'By the way, James,' said Gabriel, 'you might like to try your coat lining; I rather think Albert was right, but I don't think there are any mice. I could feel a number of things down there while I was washing your feet.'

James felt at the bottom of his coat and then he thrust his hand into his pocket, through a hole in the bottom and down to the objects concealed there. He withdrew the objects one by one – first the disputed cigarettes, then a comb and finally a couple of packs containing courtesy soap bars. He glanced first at Gabriel and then gave a sheepish look at Albert. 'Sorry, mate, I think you know me better than I know myself.' Albert nodded and grinned back at him.

James now turned to Oliver. 'Anyone who's a friend of Gabriel's is a friend of ours. What's your name, lad, and what's your problem – if you don't mind me asking?'

'I'm Oliver and I've run away from home. I love my mum, but she has nasty boyfriends and her latest hates me and is always having a go at both Mum and me, but that isn't all, because I was constantly being bullied at school and eventually lashed out at a couple of teachers. I'd had enough and then one night I had a dream and in the dream I received a message: I was to go and meet a woman who would be dressed in yellow and who would help me. Well, eventually I met up with Gabriel and here I am.'

'So sorry to hear about your troubles, but don't give up on your mum, I'm sure she loves you – what do you want more than anything else?'

'I'd love to find my dad and for our family to get back together again. I could cope with school if all was well at home.' As he said this, tears began to trickle down his cheeks.

'A fantastic desire, Oliver, pursue it with all your heart. Your family is the most important unit and well worth fighting to restore. I know this to my cost and I would dearly love to turn the clock back and do things differently. Looking at me now you probably wouldn't believe that I used to be a top accountant, but I concentrated on my job to the extent that I completely neglected my family and, needless to say, while I wasn't looking, it all fell apart – we drifted apart and eventually my wife divorced me and she got custody of our two lovely children.

'It was only then that I realised what I'd lost; I was devastated and started drinking – heavily. My excessive drinking began to affect my work and I started making mistakes, big mistakes that cost the company a vast amount of money. The inevitable happened, I lost my job and after that: no one would employ someone in the state I was in. No income meant that I couldn't keep my house. I had other debts too, so eventually I lost everything and arrived where I am today. So the bottom line is, know what's most important – care for those nearest and dearest to you – never neglect your family.'

5. Jess

What Oliver hadn't noticed was that while he'd been talking to James, Gabriel had disappeared and other homeless people had arrived. James began to introduce Oliver to them and Oliver was shocked at just how many had come from good working backgrounds. Generally all were in their present state through struggling to cope with hardships in their lives. A few were on the road through choice, though why anyone would deliberately choose such a lifestyle was beyond Oliver. What surprised him also was the fact that there were men and women of all ages – the youngest being a girl who said she was nineteen. She had an attractive face, but the woolly hat she wore did nothing to show off her looks to the best. Her clothes, too, distracted from her attractive looks – they were grubby, dishevelled and a number of sizes too big; the trouser legs she'd had to roll up at the bottom and these were resting on a pair of old Doc Martens that had seen better days. She introduced herself as Jess.

'Does anyone know where Gabriel has gone?' Oliver asked.

'Don't worry,' responded Jess, 'he hasn't abandoned you, he's in the back caring for someone who's suffering from a problem in an intimate spot. When he takes someone in there, we all know better than to barge in on him. None of us knows anything about Gabriel's background, but he's amazingly talented and I don't know what our community would do without him. He's so caring and never turns anyone away, nor judges anyone's lifestyle. So you're staying with him overnight, are you? Where does Gabriel live, and what sort of place is it?'

'It's a place similar to this, but just where it is I don't know, that's why I was anxious that he shouldn't leave me here. I don't even know what town we're in, so I've no idea how to get anywhere, especially not Gabriel's building that he calls home.'

'So where are you moving on to tomorrow?'

'You might think this is a bit strange, even a bit weird, but at the moment I don't know where I'm heading and won't do until tonight – probably it will come in a dream, though Gabriel might add a few thoughts too. My ultimate destination is one specific house that I've been dreaming about. I don't know where the house is or how to get there; I don't even know why I have to find it, though I'm told that it holds the key to my future happiness.'

'You're joking – a dream? Tell me more about the house in your dream; what was it like and what happened?'

'The house itself is nothing out of the ordinary, but it does look vaguely familiar. In the dream, I'm in the house and in bed when I'm suddenly aware of a presence: I dive out of bed and dash downstairs and through a door before whatever the presence is can catch me. I never see anyone else in the house and I immediately wake up.'

'That's amazing,' Jess responded incredulously. 'I keep getting exactly the same dream and I've been having it for absolutely ages. How can we both have the same recurring dream?'

'Wow! That sounds... er... no, not weird, exciting, and perhaps a bit scary. That's what my journey is all about: I have to find that house, though quite what happens when I do I don't know. I think it's supposed to be good, a good outcome, but I don't know what that means.'

'Well, at least you have real purpose in life; I have no purpose. I feel like I'm sinking fast. I feel like I need someone to take me by the hand and lift me back onto solid ground. I wish I could come with you; would you be happy for me to join you, if it was allowed?'

'That would be fantastic,' Oliver enthused. 'Let's ask Gabriel when he returns. He'll know what's allowed and what is not.'

'Did I hear my name mentioned?' came Gabriel's voice from behind them. 'Do you have something to ask – in fact, I'm sure you do?'

Oliver nervously explained to Gabriel, 'I've just been sharing part of my story with Jess and she says she's been having the same dreams. Jess also thinks my journey sounds exciting and wishes she could come with me: would that be a possibility, you know, would it be allowed?'

'Why do you want to go, Jess?' Gabriel asked. 'What do you think it would achieve for you?'

'I... I... er... I can't really explain,' she began. 'Yes, I think it sounds exciting, but if we can both find out what the dreams were about, that would be absolutely brilliant, and actually I've got nothing better to do and nothing to lose. I'm on my own, except for meeting up from time to time with this crowd, so it would be good to have company and a sense of purpose, even if I'm not certain what that purpose is. What it would achieve I don't know, but just as Oliver doesn't know what to expect, perhaps we can "not know what to expect" together.'

Gabriel smiled at her reasoning. 'The answer to your question, Oliver, is yes, Jess can accompany you, and in fact that was the purpose in you meeting each other today. However, I think you need to start off on the right foot – Jess, how old are you really?'

'I've been nineteen for so long now that I've almost started to believe it myself – I'm only fifteen, but I get away with the nineteen story because I'm quite tall for my age. Anyway, does it really matter how old I am?'

'Well, it's never a good thing to begin a relationship with a lie. Yes, it is both right and good for you to embark on this quest together and it will actually achieve much – future happiness for you both, and indeed for the lives of others too, lies in locating that house. What you will have to face in this quest will be fraught with difficulties, so it is good if you are not facing everything alone, as you will be mutually supportive of one another. The quest will require all the intuition you can muster; you will need to be resourceful, practical, determined, daring, yet careful. Oliver, learn to listen to the quiet inner voice you have begun to hear and trust what you hear – ignoring it could be perilous. Jess, you too will begin to hear that same inner voice and together you will be able to confirm with each other what you are hearing. Do you both understand and are you both prepared to face whatever it takes to reach your goal?'

They both nodded. 'I've come this far and I'm not about to give up,' Oliver responded determinedly. 'I feel there's too much at stake – we've got to succeed.'

'I'm totally with you there,' agreed Jess. 'We *will* succeed. Nothing and no one will stop us! I've been living rough for eight years now and I've met all kinds of creeps who've tried to hurt me and all of them have regretted it! I've learned to look after myself. We'll be OK, just you see.'

'OK, each of you take a hand and let's get back for dinner.'

They linked up one on each side of Gabriel and started walking. '

'Be at peace, both of you...'

Immediately that sense of well-being descended on them and at the same moment the pace increased till all around was a blur. After what seemed a few short moments, they slowed and approached what Oliver recognised as the building they had left earlier. They all went inside and Jess looked around.

'Gabriel, all those back in the slum reckoned you must have a posh house somewhere and you're not really as down and out as you appear, but this looks very much the same as the squat. Do you always live here?'

'When I'm on mission duty, as I am now, I do, but my real home is elsewhere. Most of the time I am on mission, though, so I don't get to spend too much time in my real home. Mission is not always in this location, however, sometimes I'm assigned to other desperately needy areas. I go where the need is greatest or most urgent. You two were the most urgent at this moment in time. Talking of needs, I guess you're both hungry. What would you like? I've got bread and cheese or I've got cheese and bread.'

They both laughed and chose the bread and cheese. They sat on the cardboard boxes to wait and Oliver took the opportunity to find out a bit about Jess. 'What's your surname, Jess, and where do you come from?'

'My full name is Jessica Amelia Patterson, but Patterson isn't my real name. I was fostered and my foster parents wouldn't tell me anything about my real mum and dad, so who they were I don't know. I was only six when I was taken into care and then fostered. I sort of remember being taken from my family home and my mum crying – I was crying too, of course, but there was a man, I don't think it was my dad, who was horrible towards me, so I was glad to get away from him, but I wanted my mum.

'I don't think I ever really recovered from all that stuff and I think that's one of the reasons why I couldn't get on with the Pattersons. I called them Mum and Dad, but I never felt they were or ever would be. I wasn't happy so when I was seven I ran away and just lived as best I could. I stole to eat, till someone from a church found me and took me to a shelter. I gave them a false name and address so that no one could send me back to the Pattersons. Eventually, the church worker took me to her home. She was very kind and caring, but when she talked about me going to school I ran away again and moved to a squat where other kids of my age sheltered. I still dream of getting back to my real home and real parents, so I'm a lot like you. My hope is also a lot like yours, that the house of our dreams will do for me what you're hoping it'll do for you. Do you think it's possible?'

'Since I've been on this journey I've met three people: the first was a woman, Marianne, then there was Joshua and now there's Gabriel, and all three have said much the same – finding that house will lead to great happiness; Marianne said I would achieve my deepest desire. Well, my deepest desire is for my family to be back together and for there to be peace and no more people like Jez around. School – I think I could cope with that now and especially so if everything was OK at home.'

Jess screwed up her nose as Oliver mentioned school. 'School! Huh! Still, I don't know, perhaps even I could cope with school if I had a happy family to support me. You know, I'd really like to have some qualifications and get a good job one day.'

Oliver reached out and grasped her hand. 'Let's do it together.'

At that moment, Gabriel came back in and passed plates of sandwiches to them both, but this time he'd provided grapefruit and orange drinks – in mugs. 'I thought it was a day to party,' he grinned, 'so I've pushed the boat out. Not only squash to drink, but also crisps and sausage rolls or cheese and onion rolls if you prefer them. Afterwards you can choose fruit, yoghurt or even sticky buns. You are free to indulge in all of the choices if you so wish.'

'Wow, Gabriel, I haven't had a feast like this in years,' Jess enthused. 'You're teaching me bad habits, but I'm so grateful, thank you very much.'

'Jess is right, Gabriel, this is a feast fit for a king; you're a real star, thank you so much.'

'You are both very welcome and I'm so glad you find my simple fare so appetising. It has been a delight for me to get to know you both, albeit briefly, but after tomorrow morning I'll no longer be with you in the same way, but you'll always be in my thoughts. I felt it was important to have a little celebration tonight, because tomorrow morning you both start on your great quest and it will end with the fulfilment of your dreams – and, I would add, even more than you currently realise or expect. I will see you again one day, as there will be a wonderful reunion and a fantastic banquet. Before that, though, you will face many trials and you will be tempted to give up, but you are both far stronger than you realise and together you will be victorious in many circumstances.

'Use your wits, stop and think things through thoroughly, don't rush blindly on – that would cause you setbacks and lead to great frustration. Love and care for each other as you would if you were brother and sister; there is strength in great relationships. One day in the distant future you will go in slightly different directions, but the bond between you will remain and you will always be special in each other's eyes.'

Both Jess and Oliver felt tears coming; they were already sensing a special bond developing between them. Theirs were not tears of sadness, but of joy they had not known before and with such a bond between them, they knew they could battle through to victory. All three of them linked hands and once more, that electric-like tingle spread through their arms and down their bodies. Who was Gabriel, and where did he really come from? Would they ever fully know him and the source of his powerful influence? As he thought about this, Oliver realised that all three of his encounters had left him with the same question, but every time he had also felt a joy in his heart, so somehow it didn't really matter. Anyway, Gabriel had said that one day he hoped to meet them again, so perhaps all would become clear on that day.

'I'm sure Oliver must have asked this question already,' Jess began, 'but how will we know which way to go to find that house? The world is a big place and we're just a tiny part of it, so will you be able to send us off in the right direction? Also, how far away is it and how long will it take us to get there?'

'Hmm, Oliver hasn't exactly asked those things,' Gabriel replied, 'but yes, I will be providing directions in the morning and will even take you to the real starting point. How far is it? That doesn't have a straightforward answer, I'm afraid. All I can say is that distance depends greatly on your focus and you using your wits, so that in turn has a knock-on effect for the time that it will take you. It will seem quite long in your time reference, but in my time sphere, it will be just moments. I'm sorry that really may not help, but be patient and all will become clear as you pursue your quest. One thing I can assure you of is this, you will reach your destination and realise your dreams – that is a given. So learn all you can and peace go with you.'

'It sounds a bit complicated,' Jess responded. 'I've never had a very good sense of direction, but when you're heading nowhere in particular it doesn't really matter. I wasn't heading for this town, it sort of found me – I just arrived. Oliver, I think it's going to be down to you to keep us on course, otherwise if it's left to me, we could end up back where we started.'

'Oh no,' Oliver responded with a gulp. 'I don't have much sense of direction either, so we could have a few problems.'

'No, don't let that concern you,' said Gabriel. 'Much of what lies ahead doesn't require you to have a good sense of direction, but rather the ability to trust and not to doubt. Oliver, just walk as your feet take you and you will arrive at your destination. This quest doesn't so much depend on the direction you take as your willingness to let someone who has your best interests at heart guide the way you walk. If you like, you're responsible for the mechanics, walking, but as regards the impetus, someone other than you will provide it. It really isn't as complicated as it sounds, but, as I've said before, listen for that inner voice, especially when you're not sure of something.'

It was quite late by the time they'd finished chatting and Gabriel suggested it was time to get some sleep. 'We've all got busy days tomorrow so we need minds that are alert and receptive: tiredness can actually block our senses, so not just tonight, but always make sure you sleep well and rest your bodies. Remember, too, you may well have relevant dreams. Anyway, your rooms, such as they are, are already prepared, so please follow me and be careful on the stairs because there is no handrail. I'm afraid the bathroom facilities are rather primitive, but everything works and I think you'll find everything you need. There is an electricity supply of sorts, but it's mainly downstairs; upstairs there's a light on the landing and in the bathroom, but not in the bedrooms, I'm afraid.'

They mounted the stairs and quickly realised that the warning had been appropriate. The worn and sometimes broken treads were difficult to cope with, so falling was a distinct possibility for the unwary. The landing above was not much better, so again, care was necessary. Jess' room was the first room on the right and the bathroom was next door. Oliver's room was at the far end on the left and the one opposite, Gabriel said, was the room he used.

Jess was amazed to find that her room was comparatively clean and there was a carpet of sorts covering the centre of the floor. Gabriel had provided and laid out a sleeping bag for her. Beside it she found the rucksack that contained all her worldly goods, something she'd forgotten about when they left the squat; she could only assume that Gabriel had brought it for her, though she hadn't seen it in his hand. Then she noticed something she hadn't expected, a pile of fresh, clean clothes, her sized clothes, a pair of new-looking trainers and even a pair of pyjamas. There was a torch by the side of the sleeping bag too – Gabriel had thought of everything. She glanced around the room; it was very basic, but it served its purpose and was far superior to many places she had dossed down in in the past.

Jess discovered later that it was much the same in Oliver's room; again, everything he needed was to hand. The bathroom was very basic, as Gabriel had said, but the floor was clean and had decent covering. There was a shower in one corner and Gabriel had provided soap and towels. Gabriel had called it 'primitive', but compared to what Jess had experienced for the last few years, this was luxury.

Jess took the opportunity to have a shower, and the warm water made her whole body feel great – she'd forgotten what it felt like to wash all over, but she wanted to be clean, ready for her fresh clothes – and who could tell when they'd next have the opportunity to shower?

Oliver heard Jess leave the bathroom and he too took advantage of the facilities.

Afterwards, as they crawled into their sleeping bags, they realised just how tired they were. It took but a few moments until both of them were soundly asleep and the sound of deep breathing filled their rooms. Later in the night, Oliver had the same dream as he'd had on previous occasions. He found himself approaching that house, but again he didn't go inside, instead he heard a quiet voice: 'Oliver, tomorrow your journey will begin and it will end at this house. As you journey, you and Jess must stay focused, don't allow anything to distract you. Remember, listen carefully, hear clearly and obey exactly. This is not a time to do your own thing. Many are the enemies to your quest, and you must overcome by using every weapon at your disposal.

'Also, remember, when you need to rest, look for the house that is provided as a place of refuge, a temporary house that will follow you throughout your journeying. Once you are inside that house no one can get to you and the house will become invisible to others. Beware, though, under no circumstances invite anyone else into the house, if you do, all protection will be lost. Remember, your enemy is very subtle and will attack your emotions. Let your resolve stay firm at all times and in all circumstances.'

Neither of them awoke during the night and when eventually they did, it was light outside. Once their eyes had fully opened, they were amazed to find that they were no longer in sleeping bags on the floor in a dilapidated old house, but rather they were in comfortable beds in a lovely house, in fact the same house, Oliver realised, that he'd stayed in with Marianne and Joshua. Oliver never ceased to be blown away by his experiences with the three wonderful people he'd encountered. Both rooms had an en suite, so they quickly washed and dressed. They exited their rooms at much the same time and Oliver looked at Jess and grinned at the incredulous look she had on her face. 'A bit of a surprise, eh, Jess?'

'You're not kidding! How could all this have happened while we were asleep? I couldn't believe it when I woke up – I had to pinch myself to be sure I wasn't dreaming. I'm still not absolutely sure.'

'You're not dreaming. I've stayed in this house twice before, in fact in the very same room, once when I was staying with Marianne and once when I was staying with Joshua; it's quite some place and it seems to appear and disappear before your eyes. Did you have a dream last night?'

'Ah, yes, didn't I just! It was a very strange dream and I saw a house, not this house and I didn't even get to go inside, instead I heard a voice giving me a message. It was all about the journey ahead, things we must do and things we must not do. Did you have a dream too?'

'Yes, I suspect it was exactly the same dream.' They went on to compare notes and they had indeed dreamed exactly the same dream. 'Jess, the house you saw was the destination for our quest, wasn't it? I'm glad you've seen all that I saw, because we can make sure we stick to the information and warnings we've had. Anyway, let's go down and see what Gabriel has to say about the transformation of our surroundings. And Jess, just look at you, you look... er... absolutely great with your new clothes! You look much better than you did before.'

'They feel good too. Those things I was wearing were far safer when living rough. I didn't want to draw attention to myself; there were enough creeps around as it was.'

'Well, you look really great now.'

'Thanks, Oliver. I feel safe enough to look more like the real me.'

They descended the softly carpeted stairs and went into the bright lounge area. A man they didn't recognise met them; he was much younger than Gabriel, clean-shaven and well dressed. He smiled as he saw the looks of surprise on their faces.

'Oh!' exclaimed Oliver. 'I was expecting to see Gabriel. He hasn't left, has he? We need some instructions for our journey and he said he would give them to us this morning and then take us to our starting point. Is he coming back?'

The man laughed aloud. 'Sorry, don't you recognise me? It's not only the house that's changed – this is the real me.'

'Gabriel?' questioned Jess. 'Wow, I'm amazed. I would never have recognised you – you look so different, so much younger!'

'Well, today I'm not going to be working with our friends at the squat, so I'm dressed for a very different assignment, starting with you two, of course. Fear not, I have your instructions ready. However, I hope staying with me has taught you an important lesson – don't judge by outward appearances; judge by the responses of your hearts – you may find you need help from all sorts of unexpected sources. In the same way, you must treat others as you would like them to treat you.'

'Gabriel, do you know about the dream we both had last night?' asked Jess.

'Yes, I was told of a message being passed to you; did you both understand it and do you realise how important it is that you heed all the warnings?'

'I do now that Oliver and I have compared notes – he's more used to these dreams and messages than I am, but I think I'm learning. We'll make sure we stay on course and do as instructed – we'll help each other.'

'I'm sure you will. Now, who's for breakfast? You can have anything you care to choose, or you can have bread and cheese.'

They both laughed out loud and gave him sideways glances.

'I think I'll go for a fry-up if that's OK,' Oliver responded. 'As great as your cheese sandwiches are, I think I'd like a change.'

'Do we both have to have the same?' Jess enquired. 'If we don't, please can I have poached eggs on toast?'

'You most certainly can, so help yourselves to cereals and there are cartons of juice on the table, or I can provide tea, coffee, drinking chocolate or anything else you may fancy. Before you eat, though, may I give thanks on your behalf?' They both bowed their heads and Gabriel prayed a most beautiful prayer of thanks to someone he obviously knew intimately and loved greatly.

Oliver had opted for a juice, but Jess had asked for coffee. They sat down at the table, poured cereals into their bowls and began to eat. What a contrast this was to their previous meal, sitting on cardboard on the floor, and indeed, what Jess had experienced during her time living rough. Gabriel brought a pot of coffee for Jess and then returned to the kitchen.

The two of them chatted as they ate and Oliver asked her about her life at the squat, but mainly they anticipated what lay ahead, what this day would bring and how they would survive when left to their own devices. So much of what lay ahead was unknown to them, and although they had both received assurance that all would be well if they steadfastly stuck to what was being revealed, they still had a niggling concern deep down inside.

Listening for an inner voice was all well and good, but what if, in the pressure of the moment, they didn't hear, or even misheard? One part of them was filled with eager anticipation at the prospect of realising their deepest desires, but concerns tempered their excitement. They were both very young and inexperienced when it came to going on a quest and, although Jess had survived years of living rough, what lay ahead of them now was completely new and largely dictated by others – even Someone who was not a tangible presence, but a presence in voice only! Were they really up to realising their goal, or would what was being asked of them prove too difficult?

Gabriel now returned with their breakfasts and placed their plates in front of them. The food looked and smelled good, and for the moment their concerns passed as hunger took control. They both expressed their gratitude and began to eat.

'All your worries are unfounded, you know,' Gabriel said reassuringly. 'Though I completely understand why you feel the way you do. You're right, this is a totally new experience for you both, but you've both already been prepared much more fully than you realise. You'll never be on your own – one of us will be on hand, not tangibly, but nevertheless definitely and deliberately to ensure you don't go off at a tangent.'

'But what about things like food and places to rest, what will we do about those things? Are we going to have to rely on what we can find in the wild?'

'Both will be covered, so you don't have to worry about either. I believe the voice in your dreams told you that when you need to rest, you were to look for this house; it will be near at hand. Once inside you will be completely safe – only you will see it. Inside the house everything will be provided, all your needs will be catered for. However, nobody will be there so you must simply help yourselves. But please remember, no one else must be allowed to join you in the house – your enemy may attempt emotional blackmail to get inside, but that would render you vulnerable – don't allow it under any circumstances. As regards food and drink for your journeying, I will give you both a pack containing all you will need and it will not run out till you reach your destination, and then the packs will simply disappear.'

'Wow, fantastic! I could have done with something like that when I was living rough,' said Jess. 'But how on earth does that work; where does the food come from, who provides it?'

'Ah, now, then, I can't explain that at this present moment, but one day you will understand – all will become clear. For now, be patient and trust and be at peace.'

6. The Quest Begins

They both quickly polished off their breakfasts. Gabriel cleared everything away and then he re-entered the room with a couple of ordinary-looking packs in plastic-like boxes. 'These are your food packs which I would ask you to include in your rucksacks. Remember, they will last right up to you reaching your destination. Now, the food provided is not ordinary food, but it will taste ordinary and the taste will resemble the foods that you like best; so eat your fill when you need to and when you come to eat again, the food will have replenished itself. Similarly, with the drinks provided: they're in ordinary-looking drinks bottles and what they contain will be whatever you're wanting them to be at that precise moment. Guard your packs carefully.'

'Gabriel, that is just brilliant,' Oliver enthused. 'It's almost unbelievable, but I know that anything is possible with you.'

'Unless you want anything more for breakfast, can I suggest you go and get together everything you need for the journey? But I suggest you travel as lightly as possible, so you can leave all that you need for each night, as that will follow after you.'

They shook their heads in utter amazement as they went back to their rooms to finish preparing and packing little bits and pieces, ensuring that their food packs were included. That done, they descended to the lounge where Gabriel was waiting; by now Oliver had a few butterflies in his stomach and the serious look on Jess' face suggested she was feeling much the same. Despite all the reassurances from Gabriel, they were stepping out into the unknown. Gabriel had spoken of the 'enemy', but what form or forms would that enemy take? They would need to remain alert and on guard just in case a strike should come – especially when they least expected it.

'It's time to move out,' Gabriel announced, 'but before we actually go, can I ask that we link hands and be quiet for a moment?' They did so and as before the tingle passed through them both and then Gabriel spoke again: 'Be at peace and go in confidence.' Both of them felt a deep sense of peace sweep over them and all the apprehension lifted. They were ready.

They stepped outside and Gabriel shut the door behind them; they started walking, but they hadn't gone more than a few steps when they glanced back and noticed that the house had already disappeared. Oliver looked at Jess and shook his head; it always amazed him how that happened. He supposed that it would continue to do so each day that they were journeying, and he hoped it would happen in reverse when they needed to rest each evening.

Gabriel's walking pace had changed to normal now; gone were his shuffling steps – the transformation was just incredible. He now took each of them by the hand and instantly they were skimming through the landscape once again. The pace was such that it was impossible to distinguish anything, so whether it was countryside or town they couldn't tell, though at certain points they wondered if in fact it was water beneath them, as the air smelled of saltwater or perhaps even seaweed. This was by far the longest journey that Oliver had experienced on any of his walks with his companions, so thoughts began to form in his mind, 'Are we going to find ourselves in some distant land, and will we even know where we are?'

Oliver's thoughts elicited a response from Gabriel, 'You're almost right, Oliver, but although it is a distant land, it's not one that you'll know or recognise. No one would know this land, but it is where your quest begins in earnest. Your encounters and experiences will be many, so keep your eyes open and your wits about you – both of you.' They both looked at Gabriel, smiled and nodded. This 'thought-talking' was something new to Jess, but she'd heard what Gabriel had said to Oliver.

'So just what are we going to face in this strange and distant land, what is really expected of us – how will we even *know* what is expected of us?'

'You'll just know, Jess,' Gabriel's response came straight back. 'You will just know, so don't worry, and simply allow the situation to unfold before you.'

As Gabriel finished speaking, the pace began to slow and before long they were drawing to a stop. Looking around, it was a rather remote-looking spot – no buildings to be seen in any direction and no sign of other people anywhere. Where they were actually standing was in a sort of large, grassy clearing, which, as far as they could tell, was completely surrounded by woodland. Oliver looked at his watch; it said 2.10pm. It had been quite a long journey, but if this wasn't England, then was his watch set right for their current time zone? 'Gabriel, my watch says it's 2.10pm, but is that correct for where we're located?'

'Yes, it is, but you don't have to concern yourselves with such a question as that, because no matter where your quest takes you, the time on your watch will automatically change according to where you are – it will always be correct.'

'It seems everything has been thought through, it's just incredible,' Jess responded, shaking her head. 'Can anything possibly go wrong?'

'No it can't, unless of course you fail to heed the warnings given. This is not a programme designed to harm you, but rather it is designed to teach you valuable lessons and ultimately to bless you mightily. You are deeply loved and very special and at the end of the quest, unlimited joy will fill your hearts. Remember, when problems do arise, fix your eyes on the goal and move confidently towards it. Now it's time for me to leave you, but before I do, I have to pass these to you.' He handed each of them what looked like a mobile phone.

'Ah, a mobile phone,' said Oliver. 'I have one that belongs to Jez, but it doesn't work.'

'No, an ordinary mobile phone wouldn't work here,' said Gabriel seriously, 'but these are not mobile phones, these are special devices – just take a look at the screen and I'll explain.'

The screens at that moment displayed a map, and in the centre of the map their current location was marked. 'These will give you your daily instructions. At the top of the screen, you will see a button marked "DAY" – please don't press it yet, as there will be nothing on the screen until I've left you. The devices will not need recharging, but think carefully through the instructions given; reason them through – you must agree things together. You will see another button marked "COMP" – that is a compass; you will need that when instructed to move in a specific direction. Finally, help each other and encourage each other whenever you feel you can't go on – nothing will be asked of you that is totally beyond your ability.'

'You didn't mention the button marked "MUS" – what's that for?' Jess asked.

'Ah yes, sorry, it stands for music; when you press that button, the music you hear will exactly fit your mood. You will find earpieces in the end of your devices; they're wireless, so they'll work even when the device is in your pocket or rucksack. If ever you drop an earpiece and can't find it, open the compass and press and hold the music button and it will locate it for you. Whenever the earpieces are back in the devices they can't fall out, so it's best to store them there when they're not in use. Do you have any final questions?' They both shook their heads. 'OK, so I must go to my next engagement.' He reached out and took their hands for a final time and again they experienced that joy-filling tingle. 'Goodbye and great blessing be yours.' He loosed their hands and started to walk away, but even as they watched it was as if he'd walked into a mist – he simply disappeared.

'Jess, it's you and me now and that's still a bit scary,' Oliver confessed with a slight tremor in his voice. 'What do you suggest we do first, any ideas?'

'Hmm, well I don't know about you, but I'm feeling a bit hungry and I don't think well on an empty stomach. I suggest we sit and have some lunch and then consult our devices; Gabriel said that they were to be our guide on the journey, so that should tell us what to do first. Anyway, I'm also curious to see how our food packs work: I fancy ham and cheese baguettes. How about you?'

'Hey, that's right, the packs are supposed to supply whatever we fancy and I fancy pizza with ham, pineapple and some tasty cheese. So let's try them out – this could be fun. I think I'll have cola to drink too.'

They retrieved their packs from their rucksacks and despite both of them actually feeling a little sceptical about it, they did in fact get exactly what they'd fancied, and how good the food tasted! Somehow whatever food they had, it always tasted superior to any they'd previously eaten and amazingly it also left them entirely more satisfied. This meal was no exception; it was wonderful in every possible way.

Their meal over, they lay back on the grass and rested, but at the same time chatted about their experiences. Oliver especially was interested to know what, if anything, Jess remembered about her early years with her biological parents.

'I really don't remember all the details; I think I've probably blotted a lot of it out, because some things were too painful and I'd no wish to relive them. I do vaguely remember my mum, she really did love me; Dad was kind, but rarely there – always working. Mum often pleaded with him to spend more time at home. Then one day he simply walked out, saying he couldn't cope any more. Mum simply broke down. Then that pig of a man came to live in our house – he was a brute and it was his treatment of me that I've blotted out. Why the authorities took me into care, I don't remember; I think perhaps I must have reported him to someone, but I can't remember the details. I think Mum would have been too scared to say anything against him. Anyway, for one reason or another they took me into care. I didn't understand what was happening, but I do remember crying for my mum later, but of course the authorities decided what would be best for me, and you know the rest of my story.'

'You know, Jess, your home sounds ever such a lot like mine, and I think you could say both situations were abusive. For me, I'm never allowed to be with Mum, even though I know she loves me. She's very weak willed and just can't stand up to the men in her life; I understand why, because I've seen her get slapped around – she's had black eyes more than once and even a broken arm. She always seems to latch on to the same sort of men and always they later turn violent. I've desperately longed for my dad to return home, but I've never even heard from him, so I can't be sure he's even still alive.'

'Do you have any brothers or sisters?' Jess asked.

'No, I… I don't think so, but I always wished I had. I would have loved to have had a brother and a sister. Especially a big sister. When I was younger I used to have a pretend sister. Sometimes I almost think she was a real person… it's almost as if she was really there. Anyway, I had fantastic fun with her, but then one day one of Mum's exes heard me talking in my room and came to see who was with me and when I told him I was pretending to talk to my sister, he slapped me hard and told me to grow up. I never talked aloud to her again, but I still pretended in my mind; it stopped me from being lonely. How about you, did you have any?'

'Well, it's strange, but in the back of my mind I always imagined that I had a younger brother, but like you I had pretend friends and family, so it could be that my memory has latched on to one of my pretend companions. The couple who fostered me had no children and neither did the woman from the church. I always longed for a family too – and I guess I still do and that's partly why I was glad when Gabriel said we could go on this quest together. I'm adopting you as my brother; I hope that's OK with you?'

'It's more than OK, Jess,' Oliver responded, 'it's a dream come true – I couldn't believe my luck when Gabriel said yes to our being together. There's only one thing that worries me: I don't want to lose you when we get to that house and it's all over. I know we can keep in touch, but that's not quite the same, is it?'

At this point both of them had tears in their eyes as they realised how, in so short a time, their common past experiences had brought them together. It almost felt as though they'd known each other all their lives and belonged together. They reached across to each other and grasped each other in a firm embrace. 'I don't think I could face what's coming without you, Jess,' Oliver confessed, 'but with you I think I can face anything – you're that big sister I never had.'

'Thank you, Oliver. We may not have known each other for long, but I see you as my brother and I'm already fond of you too. I love the way you are so open and honest; so many of the people I've met in the past have pretended to be something they're not – seeming to be your best friend, but then when your back's turned taking advantage, or even robbing you blind. If I could choose a brother, it'd be you. Gabriel said that when we reach the end of our quest, we'd have great joy: perhaps someone will take us both into their heart. So let's go for it.'

They returned their food packs to their rucksacks, at the same time locating their electronic devices and turning them on. Initially they went through the various buttons to see what each screen looked like. Eventually they together selected DAY and studied the instructions for the rest of the day. As the remaining day was comparatively short, the instructions reflected that.

Oliver read from the screen: '"Go straight ahead to the west and enter the forest; battle through until you come to the waterfall and it's there you must stay for the night, but be careful to enter the house before dusk falls; do not attempt to explore and miss the time. Danger lurks at night-time." That sounds very straightforward, but I wonder what the danger is that lurks at night-time?'

'Hmm, good question; I don't think we should wait to find out the hard way. I'm not too keen on the instruction to "battle through" either – sounds like hard work to me. I hope it's safe in that forest: we don't know what country we're in so we could meet all sorts of things in there. Did you say you had a mobile phone – why not try it and see if you get a signal? It might give us a clue as to where we are.'

Oliver felt through his rucksack and eventually located Jez's phone. 'It's not a smartphone, just a basic one.' He switched it on. 'Well, it's fully charged, but there's no signal, so either we're in another country or it's somehow blocked. I bet Gabriel wouldn't want us to be able to contact the wider world; this is a special quest and we've got to play by different rules. I think what we'll face is totally being controlled by... well, something or someone else – from another world.' He switched off the phone and returned it to his rucksack.

'Do you really think that?' Jess asked. 'What do you think the other world is? Do you mean another planet: you're not suggesting they're aliens, are you?'

'No, I don't quite know how to explain it: I think, no, I just feel that everything about Marianne, Joshua and Gabriel is somehow *spiritual*. If you think about everything we experienced while we were with Gabriel, it wasn't just natural, it was beyond belief – a house that appears and disappears at will, special food packages, even these devices – they're not like anything in our world, are they?'

'Hmm, I think I see what you mean – yes, that does make sense, but you've seen more of the guides than I have, so your experience is greater than mine. So are they trying to tell us something or teach us something, do you think? Like the dream house, for instance, why is that such a big deal?'

'I believe all of this will change our whole lives. Don't ask me how, 'cause I don't know: all I do know is that I'm getting more and more excited about it all.' By the time Oliver had finished speaking his voice level had reached such a pitch that even Jess was experiencing goose bumps.

'You're getting me terribly excited too,' she exclaimed, 'and I'm sure you're right – great things will end this quest. I want to get to the end now, but I'm beginning to realise that there's much for us to learn about ourselves and about each other, and there's also something I can't quite put my finger on. Oliver, you used the word *spiritual* when you referred to Marianne, Joshua and Gabriel; I've never thought about it, but I think I know what you mean. Gabriel's sort of different, I don't know how to explain it. *Spiritual*… yeah, but not religious… I've met religious people, and none of them comes anywhere near to what I sense about Gabriel. Is that what you meant?'

Oliver thought for a few moments before answering – spiritual or religious, was there a difference? 'That's it, Jess, I think you're right; what Gabriel, Joshua and Marianne have in common is… depth. They're *real*. But I wonder who they are, what they are, where they really come from and why we've been singled out for special attention by them, or by someone else through them?' He paused. 'Er… Do you believe in heaven, Jess?'

Jess looked a little startled by Oliver's direct question. 'I… er… I don't know; it's not something I've thought about much. I suppose it was something I thought a bit about years ago when I was taken to church by the woman who took me in, but I wasn't there for long so didn't get to know much spiritual stuff. But probably deep down I think there must be something other than this world or even this life. I don't know. How about you, what do you think?'

'I sort of remember being taught something about it when I was really little, but who by, I don't know; I think I went to Sunday school a few times… Anyway, it suddenly all stopped and there's been nothing since. Living with Jez and one or two others has taught me something about hell, though. Since I've met Marianne, Joshua and Gabriel I've been thinking about this stuff. I think they're all angels sent to us for a purpose. That doesn't mean they don't care for others too, and obviously Gabriel does, but I think their real purpose was to bring us together and send us off on this quest to find that house. Find that house and everything will become clear.'

'Angels! Do angels show themselves as ordinary people, and do they do the things Gabriel and the others have done?'

'Well, I suppose I don't know for sure. I haven't met any before as far as I know. The whole experience – there's something very out of this world about houses that appear and disappear, and gadgets like the ones we've been given; then there's food that never runs out. You have to agree, it's not *normal*!'

'Hmm, you're right...' Jess didn't sound too convinced, though she nodded her agreement, realising she couldn't entirely disagree with Oliver's thinking.

'There's something else too. I'm starting to remember some stories I heard when I went to Sunday school. I'm sure there was one story about someone having flour and oil that never ran out, and another about a man called Jesus feeding thousands of people with just a tiny amount of food and yet there was food left over afterwards. I think there were stories about angels too, but I can't remember much about them.'

Jess' face indicated some recall in her own memory. 'You know, Oliver, I think I can vaguely remember stories like that too, so I guess I must have picked them up from the woman from the church. I can't remember much, but something's lodged in the back of my memory. Wow, this whole adventure is exciting and scary at the same time, so I'm glad I'm not facing it all alone.'

They simultaneously reached out their hands towards each other and as their fingers touched, they realised what a solid bond was rapidly developing between them. They could never have expressed what they were feeling, but it was far more than just physical, it was emotional and yes, spiritual too. They had a deep affinity; they belonged together.

'Come on, Jess, the forest awaits. We may not fancy it, but it's the only way we're going to fulfil our quest and realise our dreams and who knows, it may well answer many other questions too.'

They set off in a westerly direction as instructed, heading towards the trees on the other side of the clearing. From a distance, it was impossible to determine what it would be like to push their way through the forest and to the waterfall beyond, but that was where they would rest that night. Walking on their own was vastly different from walking with Gabriel; his ability to speed up every journey was a great advantage, as it took less effort on their part. Although the grassy ground looked level and easy going, it was in fact quite tough. The grass was quite long in parts and hid many hillocks that caused them to stumble as they journeyed forwards. It took them far longer than they had anticipated to reach the edge of the forest, and when eventually they did get there they had to sit and rest for five minutes to get their breath back.

'This is going to take us far longer than I thought,' Jess said breathlessly, 'and we haven't even got into the forest yet. I can't see that there's any trodden path through it either, so I rather think it is going to be a battle.'

'Hmm, I bet you're right,' Oliver responded, 'but we'll be successful if we persevere – Joshua told me so. Remember, Gabriel said we should listen to that inner voice, especially when we're not sure about something. So do you think we should try that now, because I don't think we can simply barge through at this spot?'

'You're absolutely right – I'm so used to not having a sense of purpose that I've forgotten what it is to be focused and to plan ahead. I may be slightly older than you are, but you have so much wisdom – I most certainly need your common sense. I don't know whether listening will work, but let's give it a try.'

7. A Close Encounter

They both sat quietly on the grass and concentrated, neither of them certain as to whether they'd hear anything: How would it work, would they hear an audible voice? After a few minutes, they gave each other a questioning look. Oliver eventually broke the silence: 'Did you hear or sense anything, Jess?'

'I... er... I think I may have, but I'm not certain it wasn't just my own thoughts. Anyway, can I suggest we separately write down what we think we heard – I guess you heard something?'

'Yes, I think I did. Have we got anything to write with, or write on?'

'Yes, I have, somewhere, I did have a little notebook and pen – if I can find them.' Jess felt through her rucksack and eventually located them. She proceeded to write down what she had heard and then folded the page and passed it to Oliver. He too wrote on the page and passed it back to Jess. 'This is the moment of truth,' she said smoothing out the sheet. 'You wrote, "Walk north and a fox will show you the way" and I wrote, "Go north and a fox will lead you". Wow, that's incredible, the same message. It worked, that's fantastic!'

They climbed to their feet and set off as directed. Glancing at the forest on their left as they walked, they realised that there was not the slightest possibility of entering the trees: all the way along there was a completely impenetrable barrier of twisted, lethal-looking thorns. They'd only walked a few hundred metres when suddenly a fox, startled by their approach, rose up from between the grassy hillocks and dashed into the forest. They watched carefully where it went and turned in that direction. The barrier was not entirely broken at that point, but there was a low archway, so stooping down they were able to make their way through to the forest. It was something of a lengthy tunnel, but soon they emerged on the other side and found themselves underneath the trees.

Very little light penetrated the canopy above, so it was quite dismal. After a while, their eyes adjusted to the gloom and they were able to survey their surroundings. The forest was nothing like anything they had ever seen where they came from; it had something of a rainforest look with massively tall trees with thick foliage and from all of them hung thick vines. Despite the fact that little light penetrated to the ground, a vast array of bushes were growing, and there was no obvious pathway through.

They set off once more in a westerly direction, but it was now that they began to realise that this was not going to be a simple trek; the deeper they went the more tangled the undergrowth became, and then they began to hear noises – not those inner voices, but the noise of creatures all around them. They were having to battle not only with the forest, but also with their deepening fears within. From time to time they now came across trodden paths, but few of them led in the direction in which they wanted to go, so they expended much time and energy in fighting their way through thick undergrowth.

After the first hour's struggle, Jess at last voiced her fears: 'Oliver, I don't like this one little bit; those noises seem to be getting louder and nearer – I'm not sure I'm up to this.'

Just then, Oliver heard another encouraging sound: 'You can do it – focus and trust, be at peace.'

'Did you hear that, Jess?'

'Hear what, was it something even closer?'

'No, I heard a voice saying we can do it – to focus and trust and to be at peace.' With that, Oliver reached out his hand and grasped Jess', and immediately a peace did flow over them.

'Sorry, Oliver, I'm a bit of a wimp when it comes to jungle treks! I like my animals to be small and cuddly – those sounds didn't seem to come from little cuddly animals – I really don't fancy being a meal for some unfriendly creature.'

Oliver squeezed her hand. 'I know what you mean and I'm with you in that, but you know, I think we're safe and somehow surrounded by a protective... a sort of shield.'

'What do you mean – can you see something that I can't?'

'No, nothing visible; this is not just any walk in the great outdoors, this is a special mission and we've been assured that we're destined to succeed, so we will do it and nothing will stop us, if we do what we're told. I think I'm getting the idea that it's all about trust; learn to trust and nothing will be impossible. I don't think it's always going to be easy, but when we doubt, we're to simply trust and step out.'

'Wow, you're getting a bit deep now – where did all of that come from?'

'I think it must have been instilled in me through spending time in the company of Marianne, Joshua and Gabriel – they encouraged me to trust. So I reckon together we can do anything required of us – I encourage you and you encourage me. What do you think?'

'I'm sure you're absolutely right, but my years on the streets taught me to be suspicious of everyone and to utterly trust no one. I met so many people who were out for all they could get. You wouldn't think that people in the same position as you would steal from you, but they did – you had to keep your wits about you even when you were asleep. I do totally trust you and I would fight tooth and nail to protect you, but here in this place I feel sure we're being watched and I'm wary in case the danger reveals itself.'

'Are you talking about animals or people? Because although we're surrounded by noises I've neither seen anything nor felt we were about to be pounced on. Yes, the noises have got louder and closer, so have you spotted something I've missed?'

'I don't want to cause panic, but I think I did spot something a few minutes ago; it was only there for a split second, so I couldn't be certain that I did see something or if I did, what it was.'

While she was speaking, there came a loud crashing noise near at hand and both of them instinctively ducked down, waited and watched. The crashing continued and seemed to be getting closer. They looked around for somewhere that would provide them with cover or even protection, and over to one side Oliver spotted a very large tree with a hollow at the base: he nudged Jess and pointed towards it and together they crept in that direction. They huddled together in the hollow just in time, because at that moment a massive creature lumbered into the spot where moments before they had been crouching.

'What on earth is that?' whispered Oliver in Jess' ear. 'I've never seen anything like it – it looks almost prehistoric.' The creature was extremely large, standing at about four metres at its shoulders, but then it had a two-metre-long neck and a massive head with razor-sharp teeth. Long, thick light brown hair entirely covered its body; it was a most frightening spectacle.

The creature turned its head this way and that, sniffing the air. Could it smell them, had it heard them? They longed to see it simply lumber away, but instead it turned in their direction and began to move towards where they were hiding. Jess felt sure that the creature could hear her heartbeat; it sounded extremely loud to her. Just then came that inner voice saying, 'Stay calm, and be at peace. Those who are for you are greater than that which is against you.' She grasped Oliver's hand and squeezed it; she smiled as he looked at her and then he smiled back. She felt sure that Oliver had heard that inner voice too. Even so, the creature came up to the tree and sniffed around it and its nose poked into the hollow – its breath was acrid. It made no sign of having recognised their presence. Then the creature used the tree as a scratching post, and although it was a hefty tree, it shook with the weight of the creature's body against it. Having alleviated the itch, it moved off into the forest, much to their relief, and although they could hear the crashing noise for quite some time, it did eventually subside and all that remained was the sound of birds and other creatures in the undergrowth.

The immediate danger was over, so they crept from their shelter. How far it was to the waterfall and that promised good night's rest they just didn't know. Neither did they know whether there were more creatures like that one, or any others for that matter – they had no wish for further encounters.

'Please let there be no more such creatures,' Jess whispered.

'But what was that thing?' questioned Oliver. 'I've never seen anything like it in a zoo or in a book. Do you think it was truly real – I mean, an undiscovered present-day animal?'

'Huh, I think it was real all right, but what it was I don't know; all I know is I don't ever want to meet another one; it obviously hadn't cleaned its teeth in a while, it's breath made me feel sick, it was horrible. I suppose it could be something sent to test our nerve and resolve, but whoever sent the test has certainly got my attention and I'm firmly resolved never to tangle with anything like that ever again.'

'But we were protected and we did hear what was being said to us,' Oliver remarked. 'So I have great confidence that we can face whatever this quest throws at us. Do you think we will ever really be in danger from creatures like that one, or do you think we're protected regardless?'

'That creature was wild and dangerous and we were only protected because we listened and trusted! I'm sure that we would have been in great danger had we simply run when that thing came on the scene. Anyway, I think we need to move on; we must make sure we're at the waterfall and in the house before dark; you know what the screen said.'

They cautiously resumed their journey in a westerly direction and it just so happened that the creature had created something of a pathway through the tangled undergrowth. As they walked they both looked and listened for anything that would suggest a hidden or lurking danger. Jess' face indicated that she was not at all happy: from time to time she would briefly pause and peer into the undergrowth. Eventually Oliver noticed and asked her what was wrong.

'I'm sure we're still being watched – I just sense it. I can't say I've actually seen anything, but every so often I catch a glimpse of movement; it's only brief, a tiny flash, but I'm sure it's neither birds nor insects. I think it's human and more than one.'

'Human!' exclaimed Oliver. 'Are you sure?' It was difficult to see anything in the gloom and almost impossible to see through the tangled undergrowth. 'Perhaps it was just a breath of wind moving the leaves and both of us are so keyed up we could imagine almost anything.'

'Hmm, that maybe true, Olly – sorry, I mean, Oliver. I used to call my imaginary brother Olly, so it seems natural.'

'You can call me Olly, I don't mind. In fact I quite like that you have a special name for me. But what were you going to say?'

'Only that what I think I saw seemed to have a human form – it was only the tiniest of glimpses, but I've seen more than one, I'm almost certain.' She paused and whispered, 'No sudden movement, but glance to your right.'

Oliver casually glanced sideways just as the figure disappeared from view, but he had seen what Jess had seen; it was definitely a human form. 'You were right, Jess; it looked like a jungle tribesperson, naked to the waist and wearing a loincloth. I rather think he had a spear in his hand.'

'Let's press on and pretend we haven't noticed; maybe they'll leave us alone. At least it's easier going now that that creature has flattened some of the undergrowth, but I can't wait to reach the waterfall. What time is it, Olly?'

'Golly, it's almost 6.30, so I hope it's not much further.'

While he was talking, the track left by the creature suddenly veered to the right, so they were forced to scramble through the undergrowth. Progress was now painfully slow. They hadn't gone much further when a spear suddenly flashed past them and thudded into a tree on their left. The shaft of the spear was barring the path in front of them and they instinctively stopped and ducked down. Moments later four scantily clad, spear-brandishing hunters surrounded them. One retrieved his weapon from the tree and they all stood with spears pointing at Oliver and Jess. What were they to do now? Immediately that inner whisper came, 'Keep calm.'

'Do you speak English?' questioned Jess with a mock confident air.

In reply came a strange, unintelligible response. Clearly, they did not. Jess now resorted to pigeon English and hand gestures in an attempt to communicate: 'We need to get to the waterfall. Can you help us?'

This also failed and simply elicited another stream of incomprehensible words from the one who appeared to be either the leader or the spokesperson. However, now they appeared to want to move things along and all of them began to look more threatening, thrusting their spears towards them. 'Help!' Oliver cried out under his breath. Immediately came the inner voice, 'Speak the words that come into your mind – even though you don't understand them.'

Oliver was uncertain about this, but realising they had nothing to lose, he did as he was told. As soon as he spoke, the effect was electrifying as the tribespeople immediately lowered their spears and each fell on one knee. The leader spoke in reply, and this time both Oliver and Jess understood what he was saying.

'We wish you no harm. We were out hunting and your approach frightened away the prey. We need food to eat, so we wanted to stop you proceeding. Where are you going? What are you doing here?'

'We have been sent here and we need to urgently get to the waterfall. Can you help us?'

'We can, but first come to our village and meet our chief and then you must leave the area, so that we can hunt.'

Jess realised that refusing their hospitality was probably not a wise decision, but they couldn't take the risk of not getting to the waterfall before dark, and although it was impossible to see the sun, she sensed it was already going down, as it was quickly getting gloomier. They just had to trust that not accepting their invitation would not offend the tribespeople.

'We can't come to your village today,' answered Jess. 'We have to get to the waterfall to obtain our food, but thank you for your kind invitation; please give our greetings to your chief. So now we will leave the area and allow you to hunt. Which way do we go to get to the waterfall?'

'We will take you – follow us.' Any protest would have been impossible as they set off on a meandering course, but generally in a westerly direction. Having the guides was great, as they appeared to know the forest like the back of their hands. About half an hour later, they could hear the sound of running water and then suddenly they emerged from the trees into a grassy area beside the river, where they saw a glorious waterfall. It was indeed nearing dusk, but they had made it in time. To their right was a wider strip of grass and to their enormous relief, there was the house. It looked somewhat out of place in this setting, but to Oliver and Jess, it was a very welcome sight.

They turned to their guides and expressed their gratitude. 'Thank you for your kind help. We'll be OK now, so happy hunting,' said Jess in that unknown tongue.

'We will come with you and help you hunt for your food,' said their leader.

Oliver recognised that this was what they had been warned about; they could not allow these four to follow them into the house. It was invisible to others now, but it would become visible and render them vulnerable if they allowed them to follow them into the house. He had to think fast.

'Thank you for your offer, but our hunting is very different from yours and we have to be entirely alone; our prey has to come to us. Do you understand?'

The tribespeople looked incredulous, but then smiled and bowed before them. Jess and Oliver did likewise and the four turned and started to leave. In that split second, Oliver and Jess dashed for the door and went inside. As Oliver looked out of the window he saw the hunters standing looking back, obviously wondering how they had suddenly disappeared. Then they turned on their heels and went back into the forest.

'Wow, I can't tell you how relieved I am to be safe and secure in this place. I don't know what we'd have done without it,' said Jess. 'I'd have been happy if it had been the squat, as long as we were safe from the outside world. Anyway, how come we could suddenly speak the language back there? It seemed to take the hunters by surprise and changed their feelings towards us.'

'Yes, it took me by surprise too, but I was glad it worked. Those spears looked pretty lethal.'

They continued to chat over the events of the day, but eventually realised that they were both hungry. They saw the inside of the kitchen for the first time, and it was spotless. On the counter to one side was a message to inform them that the fridge contained two plates of food and all they needed to do was place them in the oven and turn the dial to 'Prepare', and after five minutes their food would be ready. The plates of food would become whatever it was they fancied. Jess chose fish and chips and

Oliver, chicken curry with rice. The food was sumptuous as usual and extremely nourishing. To follow, Jess chose strawberry cheesecake and cream and Oliver, apple crumble and cream. After their meal, the used crockery was stacked in the dishwasher and it was a simple matter of pressing 'run'.

Their meal over, they settled down and chatted still further, each anxious to find out more about each other and their past memories. They also read magazines that had been provided and then played board games together. It was a thoroughly enjoyable evening and both felt extremely relaxed. They were very tired after the exertion of the day, so at 10.30 they decided it was bedtime. Despite their tiredness, though, both took a while to drift off to sleep, but eventually they did.

During the early morning hours, suddenly they were awoken by a tremendous noise outside and both ran to their windows to look out. The moon bathed the scene in light and they could see a vast array of prehistoric-looking creatures obviously using the river as a watering hole. A number of them were of the same species they'd encountered in the forest and some of the larger animals were fighting fiercely among themselves. Even as they watched, the largest one of all took a vicious bite out of the neck of another and it fell writhing on the ground. It was a signal for action and other animals descended on the fallen victim and began to tear it to pieces. It took but a short time until little more than a skeleton remained. Never had they seen such a feeding frenzy.

Then to their great surprise they saw many warriors dash onto the scene and attack with their spears one animal that was grazing alone. Seconds later the creature fell, and then other tribespeople emerged with flaming torches. They formed a wall around the hunters who quickly trussed their prey and carried it off on poles into the forest. The torchbearers then retreated into the forest too, but not before they'd set fire to a number of piles of brush that had previously been gathered into heaps. The animals seemed afraid of the fires, so kept their distance. The tribe would eat their fill tomorrow.

Oliver and Jess met on the landing outside their rooms.

'I'm so glad we're safe and sound in here,' said Oliver. 'That was all pretty horrendous, but you can't help but admire those tribespeople; that was a slick operation.'

They chatted for a few moments longer and then went back to their beds, but their minds were churning and sleep didn't come easily. Oliver decided to use his wakefulness productively, so he allowed himself to look forward to tomorrow. 'I wonder where we'll go next and what we'll encounter – do we have to cross the river?' He lay there for a while and that still small voice within answered: 'Be at peace, Oliver, rest now; you do have a demanding day ahead, but the full instructions will be on your devices in the morning. Sleep, My child.' Oliver turned over and slowly and silently his mind stilled and he drifted off as though on the wings of the night, and in a matter of seconds he was fast asleep.

8. Trouble in the Air

During the course of his night's sleep, what Oliver had come to expect happened; he had a dream. This time he and Jess were outside that house and looking at it from a distance, but tonight there was something new; there were people near the house and they were all waving to them. Who they were was impossible to tell from that distance, but they waved back and then they realised that the others were beckoning them, but as they drew closer, he awoke, so he didn't get to find out who the people were. He felt some disappointment, even frustration, but it was only a dream, he reasoned.

It was time to get up, so he went and showered, dressed and prepared himself for the day, checking that everything he needed was in his rucksack. Everything finished, he left his room and went downstairs. Jess had not yet appeared, but after only a few minutes, she too came down. Oliver looked at her and realised how different she looked from the first time they'd met at the squat; there she'd been scruffy from living rough, with unkempt hair and crumpled clothes . Now she looked even more like a fifteen-year-old, with smart casual clothes, clean and with hair that shone in the morning light.

She gave Oliver a hug. 'Did you have a dream, Olly?'

Oliver shared his dream with her and Jess nodded throughout. 'It really is incredible,' she enthused. 'Our dreams are exactly the same. I really believe last night's dream is significant; I think we are going to encounter others at the house – I wonder who they are, though?'

'Hmm,' responded Oliver thoughtfully, 'if we're going to get our heart's desires, then I think it's got to be something to do with our families. So what about today? Shall we get breakfast and then see what our devices have to say to us?'

They noticed that the table had already been prepared for them with cereals, bowls and cutlery, so they went to the kitchen to get cooked food. Plates were again in the fridge and Jess opted for cheese and beans on toast, while for Oliver, it was a full English. Both chose tea to drink and they carried everything to the table. It was once again a most delicious meal and they quickly polished everything off. Having finished, they opened their devices and pressed DAY.

Jess read aloud, '"Beware, danger lurks, be alert and stay focused! Travel in a northerly direction to the gorge: cross over and proceed in a westerly direction to the rock face. Find the hidden cave – this is your passage to a bygone age. Traverse this new land still travelling westward. Your resting place for the night is the plateau." Hmm, so what do you think all that means – "a bygone age", what do you think that is?'

'Well, from what we've encountered already, I'd say it's dinosaurs! I reckon that creature we encountered yesterday and those we saw in the night belong to a bygone age, so can things get much worse?'

'Olly, this is the weirdest journey I've ever been on. Surely there must be an easier way of teaching us what we need to learn – why all these strange encounters and experiences? I just don't get it. How many more way-out things can they think up for us?'

Oliver shook his head. 'It does seem totally unreal; it's as if we're in a permanent dream. Besides the recurring dream about that house, I often have the weirdest dreams – they seem real at that moment, but looking back, I think, "What a stupid dream! Where did that come from?" This feels exactly like that, but here we don't wake up and realise that it was only a dream. But there must be a purpose behind it all, so let's stay focused and just go along with it. I'm sure it'll all become clear in the end.'

They cleared everything away, cleaned their teeth and gathered their belongings together. Oliver was just about to open the door and go out when Jess yelled at him to stop. 'We should check through the window before we go out and make sure it's safe to do so.' She went to the window to check: 'Oh, my goodness, just look at that, it's an incredible size.'

What she could see was another creature like the one they'd encountered in the forest, but this one was far larger and looked twice as menacing. 'It's coming this way and it's almost as big as the house; I don't like the look of this.'

Oliver put an arm around her shoulder. 'I think we're safe, Jess; remember, this house is invisible to all except us, so stay calm and let's see what happens.'

'But it looks to me as though it's big enough to flatten the house, invisible or not. It's coming straight at us and it doesn't look like stopping – I really don't like this one little bit.'

They gripped each other tightly as the creature approached, and the closer it got the clearer it became that it was enormous; surely nothing could stand in the path of this monster. It came right up to the front of the house, but then it was as if it had hit an invisible wall; it began to sniff the air, turning its enormous head this way and that, as if it could sense a presence – their presence. For a while, it still attempted to walk forwards, but the invisible object clearly confused it completely and it turned its massive head from side to side as if to clear away the confusing and conflicting signals. Then it turned and went around the house; they rushed to a rear window and saw it emerge and lumber off into the forest.

They both felt a tremendous relief that the ordeal was over. 'The house is our shield,' reasoned Oliver. 'It's invisible and it makes us invisible too. I'm so glad that creature didn't just tread the house down and walk right over us – that could have been disastrous.'

'You're not kidding; it was bad enough seeing it up close through the window. Whoever it was who set up this experience, they clearly thought of everything, thank goodness.'

Once again, they checked through the windows in all directions and this time there was nothing anywhere in sight. It was safe to emerge, which they now did. They checked the compass and set off in a northerly direction, following the course of the river. If there was ever any doubt in their minds as to why they couldn't cross the river where they were it was dispelled immediately; many extremely large crocodiles were to be seen basking in the sun on the sandy shore. Everything in this country seemed larger than life. Those crocodiles were an enormous risk for any creature coming to drink from the river, as they had to run the gauntlet of those vicious predators. They seemed so docile while on land, but in the water, they were an entirely different prospect, as they awaited any unsuspecting victim.

If it had been a normal walk alongside a river in England, this would have been a pleasant stroll: the sun was shining, warm but not yet hot, the grassy bank was reasonably easy terrain and the whole scene appeared tranquil. That, though, belied the dangers that lurked in the forest to their right and they were expecting some frightening spectacle to jump out any moment and confront them. They heard many sounds, including some spine-chilling roars and screeches, but so far, to their relief, nothing appeared, apart from a number of strange-looking birds flying overhead. How far it was to the gorge, they had no inkling whatsoever. Every time they rounded a bend they hoped to see it in the distance, but everything looked much the same. Mid-morning they paused for refreshments, once again choosing whatever they fancied from their food packs.

'I wish we could keep these food packs for always,' said Jess, munching on a hunk of lemon drizzle cake. 'Whatever you want whenever you need it. What could be better?'

Oliver had opted for millionaire's shortbread. 'Yeah, I totally agree, this is fantastic; beats having to buy it in a café.'

They were sitting on the grassy bank facing the river and with their backs to the forest; they were so absorbed by their snacks and in chatting to each other that they forgot to keep an eye out for possible danger. It was only when another piercing screech came from the forest that they instinctively turned to look in that direction. As they did so, they noticed that a large cat-like creature was crouching in the grass and occasionally creeping in their direction, obviously stalking them. The creature's fixed gaze was frightening; clearly, it was intent on making them its prey.

'What on earth do we do now?' hissed Jess in Oliver's ear. 'We'll never outpace it if we run and I don't fancy our chances if we take to the river. We're between a rock and a hard place.'

The answer came into their minds: 'Stay calm and perfectly still, deliverance is at hand.'

They continued to watch the animal and saw it rise up obviously ready to pounce, but even as it did so, another woolly creature, which they could only describe as bear-like, dashed up to the cat and, with one swipe of its enormous paw, sent it reeling. Before it could recover, the larger animal fastened its sharp teeth around its throat and dragged it off into the forest.

'Oh, I really thought it was going to get us, it looked so menacing as it fixed its eyes on us and when it rose up for the final pounce… wow, I thought we were goners,' said Jess with obvious relief in her voice.

'I'm still shaking,' Oliver responded. 'I can't believe we allowed ourselves to be distracted: we were told to stay focused and yet we took our eyes off the forest – we knew very well that was where the danger lay, even though I don't think we could have done much about it had we seen it approaching. I'm not too keen about being in this forest region without a guide to protect us.'

'Olly, actually we do have such a guide – in fact, a more competent guide than any human guide would be. You know, I'm learning a lot now, I never thought I would ever believe such things, but I rather like it and it could grow on me. I want to know more and I'm very willing to learn. How about you?'

'Hmm, yes, I think I am. The more I think about it, the more I believe that that's what all we're experiencing is about. Spiritual; it's something spiritual, I think.'

'I've never done spiritual in my life – well, not since I was really little,' Jess responded with a grin, 'but I think I'm prepared to give it a try. Anyway, let's get on before we get any more visitors.'

After a further half hour of trekking, they noticed that the ground began to rise and the banks of the river became considerably steeper. Shortly, there were sheer cliffs on both sides of the river. This was the gorge, but how were they meant to cross it? There was no bridge in sight and the gap between the cliffs was approaching seventy-five metres.

'I just can't see how we're supposed to get across; there's no way we could possibly climb the cliffs. Surely there must be a bridge somewhere,' Oliver groaned.

'I agree, we were told to come here to cross, so there's got to be some way of doing so,' Jess responded. She looked around for some inspiration and it was then that she noticed something that she'd previously ignored. 'Oh no! Olly, I have a nasty suspicion that that is supposed to be our bridge.' As she spoke she pointed to a thick vine that spanned the gorge, it was the only thing in sight anywhere.

'You must be joking,' Oliver responded incredulously. 'There's no way I'm going to trust that. How can we be sure it would carry our weight, anyway? What are we expected to do, use it as a tightrope, or what? No way, there's got to be another crossing place.'

'I don't think there is. You can see clearly in both directions – there's just no other way. I don't like it either, but I think we have to do it. Anyway, let's listen for confirmation.'

The confirmation quickly came: 'You can most certainly do it. Simply trust and don't doubt your own abilities.'

'Well that clinches it, I guess,' Jess responded. 'We have to go for it. I don't fancy it one little bit, but we can't stay here and the way to our goal is over there. Are you with me, Olly?'

'My heart says yes, but my mind says no way. I just don't see how we can do it, but I guess we have to try – do we sit astride the vine and inch our way across, or do we cling underneath with our hands and legs? It's such a long way across, and the idea of that drop to the river below is a horrendous thought, but I reckon if we fall we'll not know much about it. Who goes first?'

'I don't mind, I'm willing to go.'

'I think I'd rather get it over with, so if you don't mind perhaps I can go first, but I'm still not sure how to do it. I think I'll try sitting on it and shuffle my way across.'

The vine was not naturally growing in that position, but rather somebody, probably the tribespeople they'd met, had somehow managed to get it into position and anchor it with stakes at either side. It was a very thick vine and would have been extremely heavy to drag into place. It naturally sagged in the middle so they estimated that the first part of the crossing would be the easiest as that was on the downwards slope, but the second half was uphill and therefore likely to be more difficult and tiring. Oliver took a deep breath, swallowed hard and climbed onto the vine. Having his rucksack on his back was an added hindrance, but neither of them could risk losing their possessions and there was no way of getting them across other than on their backs.

Jess gave Oliver a big hug. 'Remember, Olly, you can do it and you will do it. Remember, we're determined and nothing can stop us, so let's look forward to all that lies ahead. Go ahead and don't doubt your ability.'

Oliver hugged her in return and shuffled forwards until his legs dangled over the edge of the cliff. He determined not to look down, but rather to focus on the task and look to completing the crossing. He slowly set off on the crossing, but balancing on top of the vine was not at all easy, especially as the vine moved and vibrated with every move. Once he got used to it he grew in confidence and he eventually reached the centre. He paused for a rest before he set off on the upward slope. He had only been in that position for a few moments when there was a high-pitched screeching and a giant bird-like creature swooped down on him. He ducked, and at the first pass it failed to make contact with him, but then it returned and this time it caught his shoulder and threw him completely off balance, causing him to fall sideways. He instinctively clung on with his arms, but his legs swung into space below the vine.

'Hang on tight, Olly,' shouted Jess. She grabbed one of the many stones that littered the ground around her and as the creature swooped in again, she threw the stone and it hit the creature square on the head and sent it spiralling into the abyss below. Meanwhile Oliver was struggling to get his feet back over the vine, but the rucksack was making the task even more difficult. He swung his legs backwards and forwards in an attempt to get sufficient momentum to achieve the task and just when he thought he'd never do it, he managed to get a grip with his feet. By now, though, he was thoroughly exhausted and longed to give up, but he knew he had to push himself to the limit and get to the other side. There was no way he could get back on top of the vine, so he had to continue hanging underneath.

Jess watched with trepidation as Oliver struggled, but she willed him on with every move he made. Despite the adverse conditions, the distance shortened and eventually he arrived at the opposite side. Now an even greater struggle presented itself, as he was below the lip of the cliff, but after several minutes he was able to struggle from the vine to solid ground. He lay there for quite some time not only to get his breath back and rest his weary limbs, but also to calm his shattered nerves. Eventually he climbed to his feet and waved to Jess to begin her passage across.

She moved to the vine and sat astride it; her brave and encouraging words to Oliver belied the sheer horror she felt within. She continued to sit there for a couple of minutes trying to pluck up courage to set off across. Oliver yelled across to her, 'Come on Jess, if I can do it then so can you. You will succeed, because we are going to finish this quest together and in grand style. Anyway, I need you, and now I've found you I'm not going to let you out of my sight.'

Jess looked across and nodded. She shuffled forward as Oliver had done and allowed her legs to dangle over the edge. As she shuffled still further, she crossed her legs at the ankles and began to pull herself across. The sway along the vine made her feel decidedly queasy, but she fought it back and tried to focus her gaze on Oliver. It was then that she made the mistake of looking down, and she froze. Oliver could see the fear written across her face and called out to her.

'OK Jess, you're OK, you're doing fine. Forget where you are, relax and come to me. As Gabriel would say, be at peace – let it flow over you and set off again when you're ready. You can do it.'

Jess realised just how much she too needed him – together they had a quest to complete and some answers to find. 'Yes, we'll do it together,' she told herself. Suddenly her confidence returned and she saw the opposite bank approaching, but she, like Oliver before her, found the uphill section extremely hard going. It was with enormous relief she touched the cliff face, and she threw herself forwards and Oliver helped her to crawl onto solid ground. She too lay on the ground for a few minutes to compose herself and Oliver joined her, giving her the biggest hug he could muster. They then climbed to their feet and danced a jig together – the ordeal was over so now they could resume their journey.

'Come on, Jess,' said Oliver with determination, 'let's get away from this place. I never want to face that again – I hope we never have to retrace our steps; once across that vine is more than enough. By the way, thanks for downing that bird-like creature, I truly thought I was going to plunge into the gorge. What a fantastic shot you were with that stone; I don't know whether you killed it, but it would certainly have got a massive headache. Give me our British birds and animals any time; these ones are weird and vicious.'

Once again, they took a westerly course, but this time it was not level terrain, nor easy going. Ahead of them was a high mountain and there seemed to be no way around it, as it stretched both north and south as far as the eye could see. They were only in the foothills, but rocks and massive boulders were strewn everywhere. Picking their way through made their progress rather slow. The further they travelled the steeper the incline became, and both of them were now panting for breath. They paused to get their breath back and as they did so, Oliver became aware of a rumbling noise.

'What was that noise, Jess, did you hear it?'

They listened carefully and both could hear it clearly now, and not only could they hear the rumbling, but the ground began to shake too.

'I don't think it's an earthquake,' Jess said, 'but what can it be?'

Suddenly a boulder whizzed past them. 'Hey, I think it's a massive rockslide and it's getting closer! We need to find shelter quickly. There,' she yelled, pointing to a gigantic rock to their left.

They both ran swiftly to take cover and were able to crouch at its base just in time. Initially only more of the smaller rocks tumbled all around them, but then the full force of the rockslide hit and boulders of a tremendous size crashed over and around their hiding place. Suddenly the huge rock under which they were sheltering gave a mighty lurch, and for a moment they thought it was going to topple and crush them, but instead it settled back, much to their relief. There was another ten minutes of the frightening bombardment of boulders, some of which were massive, before the slide subsided and eventually ceased; all became quiet, so they left their shelter to survey the scene. The landscape had completely changed, but their greatest shock of all was the size of a boulder that had landed just beyond their place of refuge. It had been a very real threat; its massive weight must have contributed to its speed and impetus when it struck, but now it was firmly lodged behind the one they had sheltered behind – the one that it had rocked when it had landed.

'Wowee!' exclaimed Oliver. 'That was awesome; I wonder what caused it to slide just at that moment? I really thought our refuge was going to fall on top of us.'

'You and me both: it was frightening. How many more things are we going to have to face on this journey? I don't know who thinks them up, but I wish they'd stop. Still, we're safe, and I suppose that's the main thing. One thing I'm learning; although Gabriel told us that we'd be protected, we still have to ensure that we don't do silly things and put ourselves in danger. We do have responsibility both for ourselves and for each other.'

'Yes, I thought that when I was dangling on that vine over the gorge and you came to the rescue; if that creature had come again I'm pretty certain I couldn't have held on. For once, someone cares. You're special, Jess.'

Jess hugged him once more as a tear formed in his eye and trickled down his cheek. 'If anyone treats you badly while I'm around, they'll regret it – yeah, Olly, I do care and I'll be there for you.'

It was a mutual caring love that had developed between them, and that afforded them both great feelings of warmth and well-being. What they had seemed to be natural. They were far stronger together than they had ever been apart. They would still have their individual lives to live, but they would never be exclusive lives, and what they were learning now would make all future relationships stronger and healthier. Neither of them knew what the future held for them; that was something they hoped would become clear once they reached their destination and the house gave up its secrets. One thing was certain, though – a very special relationship, the strongest possible bond, would hold them together.

They began to press onwards and upwards, now having to dodge even more strewn rocks than they had before. Occasionally individual rocks came tumbling down from above, but now all the rumblings had ceased and they were confident that the worst was over. Another hour passed and the ground levelled out somewhat, so as it was past midday they decided to stop for lunch. They found some rounded boulders to perch on and took out their food packs once more. Their lunch left them refreshed and reinvigorated, so they set off again, but before they'd travelled much further, a sheer cliff face confronted them, barring their way. There was no obvious way either up and over or, indeed, round.

'I reckon this is where the cave is meant to be,' said Jess glancing this way and that, 'but if it is, where on earth is the entrance? I can't see one.'

'Hmm, but the message did say it was a hidden entrance, so I guess we just have to search till we locate it. Perhaps it's been blocked by the rockslide.'

'I suppose it's possible, but I reckon those rocks came from much higher up and so it's unlikely they would fall in this area, but shoot right over and continue down. No, I think "hidden" simply means that it's not obvious, so it's a case of hide and seek, but where do we start?'

They moved up to the cliff face and began to walk along to their right. The sort of plateau they were on was not terribly large so it wasn't long until they reached its right-hand edge; beyond there it sloped away quite sharply, so they reasoned it wouldn't be any further in that direction, and turned back. They got back to where they'd started and now went further the other way, but reached the left-hand edge without finding anything.

'We're missing something,' Jess said with a little frustration in her voice, 'but what, I don't know. We've tried close up to the cliff, let's move back slightly and move across again.'

They moved back about three metres and started to traverse the plateau again, scouring the cliff face all over as they went. Oliver was the first to spot something. 'Hey, up there, Jess. I reckon there's something above that overhanging bit – can you see where I mean?'

He was pointing to a spot about four metres above, where the face protruded about a metre.

'Well, yes, I can see the overhanging bit, but is there a cave there? It's very small, if there is, and how do we reach it? I'm not one for scaling rock faces.'

'No, nor me, but hang on a minute, there might be a way.' He moved back to the left and found the spot he was looking for. 'Look here, there's a sloping ledge. I know it's very narrow, but it leads right up to that overhanging bit. It won't be easy, but I reckon it might be possible to climb up that way – I'm willing to try it, anyway. What do you think?'

'Huh, we've got to play at mountain goats now – you're not kidding that it's narrow, it's not even a full foot's width. We could do without having rucksacks on our backs, because they won't help us to balance. Well, Olly, if you're willing to give it a try, then so am I. I just hope it is the cave entrance when we get there.'

Oliver took a deep breath, stepped onto the lowest part of the ledge and then began to shuffle sideways up the slope. Every so often, he had to stop to look for the next possible handhold. 'Actually, it's easier than I thought,' he said. 'There are bits to grab on to, but it can't be rushed, that's for sure.' Little by little, he edged towards the top and, minutes later, he was able to step onto the overhanging bit. It was quite high, but compared to crossing the gorge, it was nothing.

'It is a cave entrance,' he announced. 'Yes, it's very small, but maybe it opens up.' He peered inside. 'Can't see, it's too dark, but there's a draught coming through, so it must lead somewhere. Wow, it's a bit whiffy, so you might need to hold your nose when you get up here.'

'That's the least of my worries,' she responded. 'I'm used to strong smells; some of the places I've lived and people I've mixed with have not smelled too sweet – do you remember James' feet?'

'Yeah, that's true,' he laughed, 'but Gabriel didn't seem to mind and he was very close up. Anyway, Jess, do come and join me, there's room for two up here.'

Jess simply grunted at him and moved to the bottom of the slope. She started to climb, but struggled at first till, like Oliver, she discovered the possible handholds. Once or twice she almost overbalanced with the weight of her rucksack, but eventually she made it, unscathed, to the top. She also tried to peer into the cave, but could see nothing. 'I see what you mean about the smell, it's very musty – I don't think it's just damp, it reminds me of something, but I can't think what. Let's go inside and see what it's like.'

9. Sleeping Giants

They both had to remove their rucksacks and stoop very low to get through the cave entrance, but a metre or so in, it did get much larger. They waited for their eyes to adjust to the gloom, but still they could see nothing further inside; this was not going to be easy.

'It's going to be a bit dodgy walking in pitch blackness,' said Oliver. 'I wish we had torches; there may be pitfalls along the way, so I don't know what we do. I wish we'd brought the torches Gabriel left for us in our bedrooms in his house. I didn't like to put mine in my rucksack; it would have felt like stealing from him.'

Just then came that inner voice once more: 'Use your devices.'

They both reached into their rucksacks, retrieved their devices and switched them on. Much to their surprise, not only did they give out light, but also it was infrared light.

'That, I have to say, is a great relief,' said Jess, breathing deeply. 'I'm not great in the dark anytime, but in this place it might well have been disastrous. Who knows what we might encounter. I like to know what I'm up against before it hits me.'

'I know what you mean,' Oliver agreed. 'I don't mind the dark if I'm on familiar territory, but this just isn't and that smell seems to be stronger now we're inside. I think it smells like an animal. From what we've seen already, I hate to think how big and how ferocious it might be if it's in its den. I think we should be as quiet as possible so that we don't too readily warn anything of our approach. Fortunately, I think I've heard that animals can't easily see infrared light, so if that's true then we have the advantage; we can see without anything seeing us. Are you ready to go on, Jess?'

Jess gripped his hand and they moved slowly forwards. The light from their devices was not particularly bright, but it was sufficient to enable them to make out any obstacles along the way – boulders on the floor, protrusions from the roof and walls and also the occasional hole. Without the light, it would have been an impossible journey. There was no way of knowing how long the tunnel was, but the size of the mountain suggested that it would be quite a distance. There certainly was no distant light to suggest they were nearing the exit; however, that could also be because the tunnel was not straight, but changed direction from time to time. What concerned Oliver more than anything, though, was the fact that the stench was getting stronger and stronger; were they at any moment going to encounter some prehistoric-looking creature?

They'd been walking through the tunnel for about forty-five minutes when they heard snuffling and snorting, but there was so far nothing visible. They now moved even more cautiously, anxious not to stumble unexpectedly onto some sleeping creature. The stench by now had reached a nauseating level, even for Jess, so both used handkerchiefs to cover their noses. They rounded another bend and now they could see the source of the stench: lying there were two giant bear-like creatures. These were no ordinary bears; to start with, even in that prone position they looked as big as elephants, their paws were enormous, bigger than basketballs with long, dangerous-looking claws, and they were covered in thick, long hair all over. They were a frightening spectacle and their bodies blocked the passageway. So far, they appeared to be completely unaware of Jess and Oliver's presence, something they were anxious should not change.

'They're absolute monsters,' whispered Oliver in Jess' ear. 'How on earth do we get past them without disturbing them? I don't fancy being in here if they suddenly wake up! We wouldn't stand a chance against them.'

Jess shuddered at the thought. 'Maybe we have to wait for them to wake up and hope they then leave the cave.'

'I don't think we can do that – they probably go out at night and we have to be safely in the house before dark. No, we have to think it through; there has to be another way to get past them.'

They began to scan their surroundings for a solution and they noticed that the cave at this particular point had opened up into a high-vaulted cavern. What options did it offer other than the obvious one of attempting to creep past the sleeping creatures? And this was not really an option, as they were certain it wouldn't be possible without disturbing them and risking certain death. As they looked upwards towards the roof, they noticed in the gloom that there were many bats hanging there; if they were to disturb them, would they in turn disturb the creatures and tempt them to leave their den now? Once again, it was an unlikely scenario, so they dismissed the idea. Eventually Jess came up with a viable solution, after she had walked right up to the left-hand wall.

'Olly,' she whispered. 'Look at this.' She pointed to a ledge very similar to the one they had used to climb up to the cave entrance. This was about half a metre from the floor, but a short distance along, it rose to about two metres. It was impossible to say whether it ran the full length of the cavern, as the light was not strong enough to see. They could only risk it and trust that it did.

'I'll go first this time,' she whispered. She stepped up on to the narrow ledge and found that it was actually narrower than their previous climb. Handgrips were difficult to locate, but very slowly she inched her way along. Oliver gave her quite a head start before he stepped up and began the journey, but he too found the going extremely gruelling – tiring on the feet and painful to the fingers. Halfway across, Jess almost fell as she stepped sideways and the rock gave way beneath her foot. A chunk of rock, the size of a football, rocketed down and struck one of the creatures on the head. Jess and Oliver both saw it hit and stopped in their tracks, holding their breath. The creature rose up on its front paws and gave a mighty roar. The sound ricocheted around the cavern and scattered the sleeping bats. The flapping of wings filled the air, resulting in the second animal rising up and adding its voice to the terrible cacophony.

The noise died down, but then the creatures began to look around for the reason they had been disturbed. Although they sniffed the air, and especially in the direction of Oliver and Jess, they didn't seem to detect their presence. To their relief the creatures settled down again, but Jess and Oliver waited a few moments before resuming their journey. Jess soon reached the other end of the cavern and with great relief was able to step down onto the floor of the cave. Oliver continued along, and when he came to the point where the ledge had given way, he made sure he stepped well clear of the gap. He too safely completed the crossing, and, like Jess, was mightily relieved to be able to step onto firm ground again. It took only a few minutes to traverse the rest of the cave and to their great relief they soon saw daylight ahead. They turned off their devices and stowed them safely in their rucksacks.

They stepped from the cave into the evening sun and the sight that met their eyes simply left them breathless. This was indeed a bygone age – literally a prehistoric landscape that stretched out before them. They now stood just outside the cave on a large plateau, larger than the one on the other side, and this one was level and largely free of boulders. But it was still rocky ground and this, they realised, was most likely where they were supposed to spend the night. They looked around, but there was no house in sight, so they concluded that perhaps it was not yet time. Providing the two bear-like creatures didn't emerge, they decided this was the ideal opportunity to scan the land before them. The plateau was quite high up, so they were able to look down on everything. The land before them was vast and was roughly circular in shape, a sort of bowl completely encircled by high mountains. The most likely explanation for its existence was that it was the crater of a vast extinct volcano; how the animals came to be present was anybody's guess. It was an amazing sight and probably had its own microclimate. Yes, it truly belonged to a bygone age, but it was their privilege to see it for real. Did this place really exist in the twenty-first century? Surely, they were simply glimpsing a scene from the past. For now, though, it was real, but what exactly 'real' meant for them no doubt they would eventually discover.

'This is absolutely amazing,' said Oliver. 'It's as if we've stepped back in time – these are creatures we've only read about, and yet here they are alive and walking the earth.'

Both flora and fauna were so different from anything they'd previously seen in real life: there were many animals they recognised from pictures they'd seen, such as tyrannosaurus rex, triceratops, stegosaurus and some mammoth-like animals with long curved tusks, but should they have been here along with the dinosaurs? Many other creatures they recognised but couldn't put a name to. There were numerous flying creatures too. 'This is absolutely crazy,' said Jess incredulously. 'It feels as though I'm dreaming and any moment I'm going to wake up.'

They continued to gaze at the scene, pointing out different things as they spotted them. 'Hey, look over there, by that wooded area! People – and they're stalking that deer-like animal, but will they get it before it spots them?' Even as they watched, more hunters rose up from the bushes, and the startled animal ran towards the other hunters. The animal saw the other hunters, but before it could take evasive action, one man threw a spear and it pierced the animal in the neck, causing it to tumble forwards. All the hunters then piled in and the quarry was quickly killed. That, no doubt, would be dinner for the tribe that night.

Jess and Oliver now turned their attention to getting into the house. The sun was disappearing below the hills in the distance and the matter was getting urgent, but still the house was nowhere in sight.

'I'm getting a bit concerned,' Jess confessed. 'I'm sure it should be visible by now. I don't fancy spending the night in the open, especially if those two brutes emerge from the cave. Help, somebody!'

Help immediately came in the form of two simple words, 'Look around.'

'We're in the wrong place, Jess, this isn't the plateau that was meant! It's that one over there.' Oliver pointed to a level grassy plateau about 400 metres to their right. There the house stood ready to welcome them and provide them with protection. As they gazed in the direction of the house, they noticed that a herd of creatures was moving in their direction and soon would stand between them and safety.

'Come on, Jess, we have to make a dash for it; that herd may not be friendly and they'll soon cut us off. Do we run and risk attracting attention, or do we keep low and move carefully?'

'To be honest, I think we do both. I don't think we'll have time to move too carefully, but I think you're right, we stay low, but we make a dash for it.'

With that they set off and used every bit of cover they could to try to disguise their movement. None of the creatures seemed to notice them until they'd covered about three-quarters of the distance, then seeing movement, they began to rush in their direction. It would be touch and go as to who would win the race, so now there was no purpose in staying low, speed was of the essence. The last 100 metres was uphill, but there was no possibility of slowing down, so they pushed their tired limbs to the limit. They reached the house only twenty-five metres ahead of the herd, but they were able to dash inside and slam the door just in time. The herd came to a sudden halt as they encountered the shield around the house. Looking through the window, Oliver and Jess could see the herd, about fifty strong, standing there, snorting and snarling. Their quarry had vanished and clearly they were not happy, so now they began to turn on each other and the resulting fights were both noisy and vicious.

'Wow, am I glad we got inside when we did – just look at those jaws! I wouldn't want to be on the receiving end of those,' Jess said. 'They're tearing chunks out of each other now; they just don't give up, none of them are willing to retreat.'

'I don't know how those humans we saw cope in this place; they must live in fear and trepidation every single day. A spear would be of little use if that whole herd ambushed you; I wouldn't even want to face them with a gun in my hand.'

'Talking about hunting and feeding,' said Jess, changing the subject, 'I'm hungry and I think we should go and hunt for our evening meal; what do you say?'

'Good thinking, but I think I'll have mine cooked, please! I'm not going out there again.'

The table, they noticed, was already set out for their evening meal, so they went through to the kitchen to get their food – chicken casserole with peas and a jacket potato for Jess, and gammon steak, egg and chips for Oliver. This house was a dream: no shopping, no preparation and no washing-up; even the food was prepared in a matter of seconds. Only moments later, therefore, they brought their food through to the table to eat. Neither of them could remember when they'd had such meals at home.

'Olly, I think we should give thanks for everything, just like Gabriel did; I've never done it before, but somebody very kindly provides for all our needs and also watches over us, so let's say thank you.' They both bowed their heads and Jess said a very simple thank you for their safe deliverance and the wonderful provision. The way Jess had spoken, left Oliver feeling deeply impressed and he felt joy and thankfulness well up within him.

After their fantastic meal together, they sat together for the rest of the evening and chatted over the events of the day. It didn't stop there, though, as they eventually moved on to share together all they were learning, and there was much to say. Neither of them was the same person who had started out, they were both much stronger emotionally and more confident about facing whatever came their way. They also began to share anticipations for the future – what finding that house would eventually achieve and where their lives might go from there. They shared their hopes, their dreams and their ambitions. One thing they were totally in agreement over: their futures definitely included each other; they'd come together, they'd struggled together and nothing was going to stop them being there for each other, no matter what and how their lives might diverge.

They were thoroughly exhausted by the time they went to bed that evening and both were wondering, 'Will we dream?' and 'What will tomorrow bring?' Clearly, they would have to negotiate this prehistoric landscape, but what would they encounter and where would they be going next?

Although Oliver was desperately tired, the experiences of the day were still swirling around in his mind, so he was tossing and turning for quite some time. He tried all the many ideas that people in the past had suggested for getting off to sleep, like counting sheep or focusing the mind on very tranquil scenes, or the waves of the sea. However, nothing worked. Suddenly it came to him, something he'd not done so far; he turned on his device, inserted his earphones and pressed MUS. The gentlest of music began to bathe his senses, and in a matter of minutes he drifted off into deep, refreshing sleep. He did dream and, once again, he was standing outside that house. He couldn't see anybody, but he sensed something was happening inside – preparation. The only words he heard were, 'Just two more tests and then you enter the land of promise.' He didn't wake up, though, and the next thing he knew it was morning. The serene music was still playing so he switched off the device and stowed the earphones. He felt wonderfully refreshed and raring to go. The message of the night had given him fresh urgency of desire: he wanted to complete the journey. He wondered whether Jess had heard it too. He packed his device in his rucksack and went to the en suite to shower.

He had just finished dressing and preparing when Jess knocked on his door. 'Are you decent? Can I come in?' She waited for his confirmation and entered. 'I just couldn't wait to ask if you'd heard a message during the night.'

'I surely did. Great news wasn't it?'

'Fabulous! I'm feeling rather excited, as though the end of the quest is near. I know we still have a couple of tests, but after what we've faced already, I reckon I can cope with two more. It's made me hungry too, so come on, let's go and eat.'

They went down together and both chose an enormous fry-up, with toast and marmalade to follow. As they'd had cereal to begin with, it really was a very hearty breakfast. Throughout their meal they chatted animatedly, such was their excitement, but then Oliver eventually brought them down to earth.

'You know, Jess, although I'm greatly looking forward to getting to that house and finding out what it's all about, I am going to miss our times together: you're the best thing that ever happened to me and I don't want that to end.'

Jess jumped up from her chair, dashed round the table and flung her arms around Oliver. Tears flowed liberally from both of them.

'Olly, I promise here and now that no matter what the future holds for both of us, I will do my best to make sure that we still spend special times together. I don't want them to end either. As far as I'm concerned, you are my dear, dear brother, in fact, the dearest possible brother.'

They continued to hug for quite some time; the bond between them was powerful, deep and strong. Their pledge was not just some emotional, spur-of-the-moment feeling, it was genuine and sincerely meant. Theirs was a commitment that mutual struggles had sealed and no doubt, the coming days would strengthen it still further.

As they realised this they also realised that they really ought to see what the day's instructions had to say.

'Oh wow!' exclaimed Oliver as he read from his device. 'Today will be a day of battles. Be alert and on your guard at all times. You will have great success, provided you listen carefully, plan strategically and keep your eye on the goal – the triple peaks. Generally, you will still journey westward, but determine together the best route. Pass from this land through the golden gate and rest on the banks of the waters.'

'Goodness, what does all that mean? The problem is, we can't ask questions; or can we? Perhaps we can – that may be why we need to listen carefully,' reasoned Jess.

As she finished speaking, the answer came: 'Got it in one!'

'Wow, what a system,' said Oliver in response. 'I wish that inner voice could be with us always, it's such a fantastic help.'

Again came that inner voice: 'What makes you think it won't be? It will be up to both of you to ensure that the spiritual airwaves stay open, you maintain a daily relationship with the Speaker, and you continue to want what is best for you. You will fully understand in a few days' time when the final revelation comes to you.'

Both were wide-eyed with wonder as they began to speculate as to what that final revelation might be, what it would entail and how it would affect them. They recalled too what they'd been assured would be the final outcome of the quest – the deepest desires of their hearts would be realised. What now were their deepest desires? Both were aware that their desires had progressed, changed, developed during their time together and the experiences they'd had, so could they now hope, dare to believe, truly expect that all their new desires would be realised? No, they couldn't allow themselves the luxury to dream their dreams aloud in case there was disappointment. They'd just have to wait and see.

10. A Bygone Age

It was time to get started, so they cleared everything away and went to their rooms to make their final preparations for the day. They always had to make sure that everything they needed was included in their rucksacks, especially their devices and food packs. Everything checked, they went downstairs and over to the window to look out. The sight that greeted them was incredible. The creatures that had been present last night were still there, but their numbers had swelled greatly; it was as if they'd called up reinforcements. Did they somehow know that their quarry was still there? Certainly Oliver and Jess couldn't be seen, but could the creatures sense their presence?

Jess shook her head in total disbelief. 'No way am I going out among that lot! It looks to me like it's become personal and they're out to get us.'

'I'm totally with you in that,' Oliver responded, 'but somehow we have to be able to get past them and pursue our course. Any ideas, Jess?'

'Do you think they'd respond to us politely asking them to leave our front garden? No, I really don't have any ideas, except that I think we should ask for help.'

They paused with that cry from their hearts and the answer quickly came: 'This is the first battle: go out, shout and run at them. Victory is yours.'

'Did you hear what I heard, Olly – shout and run at them?'

'That was exactly what I heard, but I have to say I don't fancy it; they look pretty vicious to me and I can't see them being frightened of us.'

The voice came again: 'You are not alone, open your eyes and see.'

They looked out again and what they saw now was amazing – yes, the creatures were still there, but now there was also a long line of massive men with what appeared to be flaming swords in their hands. 'That is incredible! Who are they and where did they come from? They weren't there earlier,' said Oliver.

'I wonder,' responded Jess. 'Maybe they were there but we couldn't see them till our eyes were really opened. I think this is another of those spiritual happenings. Well, I'm confident that victory will be ours, so let's go.'

They stepped outside and the creatures all turned in their direction and looked as though they were about to charge, but suddenly seemed to think better of it and began to step backwards. This was their cue; they began to shout and run at the mighty herd, and the warriors ran with them. The warriors seemed to be about two and a half metres tall and the creatures knew it was time for a sharp exit. They turned tail and with mighty roars ran in the opposite direction; they didn't stop, and Jess and Oliver them until they were a distant speck. They could no longer see the warriors, so whether they were still in pursuit it was impossible to tell.

Oliver and Jess gave each other a high five. 'Fantastic!' exclaimed Jess. 'I just can't grasp how these things happen, but I'm willing to learn. I like having a helper to hand. I really am beginning to want to know more, to understand more and to experience more. I'll be honest, I've always written religion off as meaningless mumbo-jumbo, but this is… different, this is exciting – alive, powerful and real! Thank You, whoever you are, for sending us the help we needed.'

'That's right, Jess; these experiences give me goose bumps. I hope when we get to that house it's not just a happy ending but we can understand more. Yep, like you, I want it, whatever it is. It's all very exciting. I can hardly wait. My mum will never believe all this when I tell her! Oh, and Jess, I reckon Mum will love you.'

Hugs had become a normal response for them, so right there and then they threw their arms around each other. Then they started to journey again and set off in a westerly direction. Before they'd gone far they remembered what the last message had said about planning strategically and fixing their eyes on the goal. 'So can you see what we're heading for,' asked Oliver, 'triple peaks, it said?'

'There certainly are mountains in the distance, but more than three peaks, so which ones does it refer to? They seem to me to all be too far apart for us to fix our eyes on; I think we must be missing something.'

'So why do you think we can't just go west in a straight line, that would be the quickest and shortest route?' Oliver asked questioningly.

'Hmm, I was wondering about that,' Jess responded, 'but the more I think about it, there aren't many creatures roaming the plain before us right now, but that could quickly change and we don't want to put ourselves in danger if we can avoid it. I think that area in the centre is marshland; I can see a number of pools and I think there are reeds growing in that area too – not a wise place for us to go. That, I think, must be why we have to plan strategically, but if we veer away from our straight line west we need a focus point to bring us back on course, so I reckon there must be another triple peak that we've not yet spotted. So where is it?'

Both scanned the distant horizon and for quite some while couldn't spot anything that was likely, but then Oliver retrieved his device and pressed COMP – suddenly it was clear that they hadn't been looking in a true westerly direction. Now they could see the triple peaks, and they realised they were not mountain peaks at all, but were in fact three spikes of rock that looked rather unnatural from this distance.

'Well, I suppose that makes it clear we need to go round the left side; that takes us near to the wooded area and there might be lots of wild animals in there. There aren't many creatures around now, that's true, but that probably means that they come out to hunt in the evening and that's why we saw so many last night. Mind you, it doesn't mean they're all asleep. They might quite fancy a daytime snack. We really do need to stay alert and ready for whatever might come our way,' Oliver reasoned.

'It's just occurred to me that the route we're taking will also take us near to where we saw the hunters last night. I wonder how they will react if they spot us? We'll look strange to them – they could prove hostile,' Jess warned.

'I was just thinking about that myself, and the dreams that started this whole adventure came to mind,' said

Oliver. 'How did you feel about your dream? What did you imagine was happening?'

'Well, I was absolutely scared to bits and just wanted to run away from… what? I suppose I imagined it was some vicious creature, a monster, something out to get me. But why do you ask, what was your reaction – you had the same dream?'

'Exactly the same as you. Now it makes me think that this is probably what this experience is all about – we're facing the unknown. We don't know what lies ahead of us today, so our natural reaction will be to run away from anything or anyone who appears hostile. Now I know there's a difference, because in our dreams we saw nothing – we didn't stay to find out what it was we were frightened of, whereas here we'll see whatever attacks. What if we hadn't run in our dreams – would that "presence" really have been hostile?'

'I don't know where you're going with this, Olly; does it have some connection with today and how we react to a real presence?'

'Yes, that's what I'm wondering: it's natural to run from danger, but there may be times when it's right to find out if there is real danger before we run. I'm not suggesting we tangle with vicious animals, but I suppose I'm wondering how we react if those people we saw should ambush us. Those tribesmen we met the other side of the gorge turned out to be OK when we spoke to them in their language, so I think we should attempt to talk to the warriors here, if they should capture us. But it may be a problem if they attack first and ask questions later!'

They had been talking as they walked and had covered a considerable distance when suddenly there was a terrible screeching from above and two pterodactyls swooped down with vicious claws extended in their direction. Jess and Oliver immediately hit the ground and hoped that the creatures would leave them and seek other prey, but they circled and came in again. This time Oliver was ready and he lifted his feet and kicked one of them hard. He made a solid connection and the creature flew off, wobbling in flight as it did so. It didn't deter the other, though, and once again it swooped in and this time both attempted to kick it, but it skilfully evaded them both. Before it could turn and come again, that inner voice rang in their minds: 'Stand up, raise your arms towards the attacker with palms forward and command it to "STOP".'

This was surely very unlikely to be successful, but both had heard the same instruction so obeyed instantly. As the creature came in, Jess counted, 'After three, Olly – one, two three!' Simultaneously they jumped to their feet and shouted 'STOP' and to their great amazement and relief, it veered to one side and flew away.

'Absolutely incredible,' breathed an amazed Oliver. 'I'll never get used to how these unlikely things happen. How come that worked? It shouldn't have, but I'm so glad it did. I suppose that's sort of what I was trying to say earlier; there are times when running seems the normal thing to do and yet staying put and doing the unexpected is the thing that actually works! I feel as though I'm trying to explain the unexplainable, but hopefully you understand a little bit of what I'm trying to say, even though I'm not saying it very well.'

'Yes, I think I do understand, because that was what we did just then and we had that victory. Anyway, come on, we've still got a lot of ground to cover: it's far from over yet.'

They continued to skirt the woodland as they traversed the curve that would eventually lead them to the triple peaks. The nearer they got to those peaks, the less they appeared natural. They could only assume they had a purpose, but what purpose it was impossible to know: maybe they were a tribal shrine, or perhaps they had some practical use. They might never find out. Across the plain there were a few creatures roaming and grazing, but none seemed to be interested in Jess and Oliver, and that was fine by them. Soon after midday, they stopped and sat in the shelter of a gigantic rock to eat their lunch. It was good to rest and suddenly they were aware of how hungry they were. All the time they were in that place they didn't make the mistake of ignoring what was going on around them, as they had the day before. Occasionally one or the other would rise and take a good look around, but there was nothing to concern them near at hand.

They had just finished their meal and were packing everything away when they felt the rock move. Their immediate thought was that perhaps the volcano was not as extinct as they had imagined, and that the movement was the result of a ground tremor. The rock moved a few times and, slightly alarmed, they stood to their feet to see if some creature was moving it from behind, perhaps using it as a scratching post, but there was nothing there. Then before their eyes, the rock rose from the ground on four legs and a head poked out at one side. It was a giant tortoise-like creature and now it turned its head in their direction and showed rows of sharp teeth. Their initial instinct was to make a sharp exit, but they were both somewhat intrigued and stood motionless. It did not appear hostile and eventually, having given them the once over, turned away and began to munch the vegetation.

'Now I've seen it all,' laughed Jess, 'a rock on legs. I suppose it's sort of like an overgrown pet, quite cute in its own kind of way, but it certainly came as a shock when its feet and head appeared! Things aren't always as they seem here.'

They did, in fact, see other strange creatures from time to time, a millipede about a metre long scurrying between the trees and giant lizard-like creatures the size of crocodiles.

'Everything's so big in this place, they don't seem to do "normal" around here,' said Oliver. 'There's a lot to be said for the animals back home.'

By mid-afternoon they'd made excellent progress and they were beginning to anticipate reaching their goal, when the air was split by great yells and grunts and they found themselves once more surrounded by spear-waving men. They all looked enormously strong and were very intimidating. The men thrust their spears towards them, indicating that they were to turn and walk to the trees. They didn't attempt to protest, as they were in no doubt that the men were serious, so Jess and Oliver decided that talking could come later.

They went deep into the forest and eventually entered a clearing where makeshift shelters were dotted around, many of which were occupied by women and children.

Their rucksacks were taken and they were ushered to one shelter that was much larger than all the others. There they found themselves face to face with a man who looked even bigger, stronger and more intimidating than the others. This, they reckoned, was the chief. He motioned them to the floor before him and then much incomprehensible chatter took place between him and the other men. Eventually the tribesmen prodded Oliver and Jess to their feet with their spears and then walked them to the edge of the village and tied them to a tree.

Oliver was still facing the centre of the clearing and he could see that there was much animated discussion taking place. Eventually he realised that they'd reached some sort of conclusion and the men came back, untied them and took them into the centre of the village again. The warriors made it clear that they had to kneel on the ground, but this time they were in the open and as the warriors with spears approached, it was clear what their intention was.

Now they needed help. The voice told them to speak out with authority. Jess tried, but at first without success, so she paused and then tried again, yelling, 'Stop!' This time the men stopped and listened, seemingly amazed that they were hearing their own language. 'Do you men know who we are?' Jess asked in the most authoritative voice she could muster. 'We have been sent by a very high power to this country and that high power demands that you release us and send us on our way, or disaster will strike you.'

Oliver felt compelled to join in: 'Giant hailstones will rain down on you all and you will be killed and your bodies given to the wild animals.'

'Silence!' ordered the chief. 'Where are you from and why have you come here? What is this strange covering you have on your bodies?'

'All you need to know is that a mighty power who controls all things has sent us and this covering you ask about is for our protection from all harm. Heed the warning, all of you, or your lives will be forfeited!' said Jess, picking up the threads again.

Then, much to their alarm, they realised that the warriors intended to test their protective covering – not, it seemed, with the use of the spears, but by presenting them as an offering to the animals. Was that really better than the spears? They were now forced back out of the forest and then to the rock pinnacles. Suddenly they realised why they were there – they were for the offering of sacrifices. They tied victims to the rocks and offered them as sacrifices to the wild creatures roaming beyond. It was now their turn; they were tied to a rock and then the men withdrew to the trees to watch. No doubt this was a regular occurrence, because after just a few minutes a number of very vicious and hungry-looking predators moved speedily in their direction.

It was time for action and both cried out for help and having done so awaited their fate. They didn't have long to wait, because suddenly the creatures stopped in their tracks and started to back off, snarling as they did so. Moments later the creatures ran away at speed. They both began to breathe deeply, mightily relieved at their deliverance.

That was a signal for the men to give a great yell and then they rushed to release them. Once again, they were ushered to the village and the happening reported to the chief. Now suddenly the tables were turned and all the tribespeople fell on their knees before them, and this included the chief. Oliver and Jess encouraged them back to their feet.

The chief now offered them safe passage, urging them to leave and pleading that they take back the terrible threat of destruction. They agreed to leave and promised that destruction would not now happen to the tribe; finally, they insisted that the men return their rucksacks, and this was obeyed without any protest. Now the men escorted them to the edge of the forest and as they walked away, they noticed that the brave warriors were bowing in awe and wonder. They were extremely relieved to get away and so grateful for the help they'd received from that still, small voice.

'We're free,' Oliver remarked, 'but we can't leave the area, as this is where we're supposed to find the golden gate, whatever that is, and that's where we leave this bygone age. Any ideas, Jess?'

'Hmm, that's a good question. Ever since we got the message this morning, the golden gate is something that I've been thinking about. It has to be near here and as that tribe is here too, I wonder whether there's a connection. I don't think I fancy asking them about it, so we'll just have to find it for ourselves.'

'I'm certainly not going to try asking them,' Oliver growled. 'I don't want to push my luck with them ever again. Thinking about the golden gate, I reckon it has to be somewhere on the mountain on the other side of the forest – it has to be a cave and tunnel through the mountain like the one we came in through. But how do we find it – how do we get through the forest and past the village without being spotted?'

'That is a good question, Olly. The only thing I can think of is to go around the village, say to the right from here, and giving it a wide berth. If we can successfully find our way through to the mountain and then move left again, maybe we can somehow get to the gate.'

'I'm up for that,' responded Oliver, 'but I just hope we don't meet anything else on the way.'

With that, they set off, initially travelling north, and after a short while, they turned west and entered the forest. From here, they really needed to stay alert and observant: nowhere could they be certain that they wouldn't run into man or beast. They were immediately aware of noises and movement somewhere around them, but for the most part, they couldn't detect which direction the sounds were coming from, and nothing appeared. The further in they penetrated, the louder the noises got, and they became convinced that large animals lumbering through the undergrowth were the cause of some of the sounds.

'Hold it a minute, Olly,' whispered Jess. 'I think something's heading our way. We have to find somewhere to lie low.'

They looked around, but there was no immediately obvious place, so they turned south for a few metres and came upon some rocks. A tangle of vegetation partly hid the rocks. They were able to push their way beneath the cover, and there they waited. Moments later, a giant creature came into view. It was in fact a spinosaurus with a long neck and tail. It stood still, sniffing the air, turning its massive head this way and that as though trying to locate the source of their scent. It was then that their worst fears were realised, and much to their horror, it came towards them.

Its long neck stretched in their direction as it came closer. They slowly and quietly moved around to the opposite side of the rocks, hoping that it wouldn't detect their movement. Its massive head and powerful jaws probed the undergrowth near to them, but then to their great relief it gave up its search and finally retreated, continuing its passage through the forest. Danger past, they crept from their hiding place and, making sure there were no other predators around, continued their journey. It was far from easy going, as the undergrowth was extremely thick in places. Every so often, they had to dive for cover as more creatures came along. It was a nerve-racking journey. They encountered many smaller creatures, such as lizards and flying mammals, but these were easier to avoid.

Jess was not a lover of creepy-crawly things and for her this journey approached something of a nightmare. 'Oh, I'll be so glad to get away from this place,' she groaned. 'Why anybody would choose to trek through forests beats me. I will most certainly have horrible dreams tonight. Ugh, get off,' she cried, brushing off a huge spider that had dropped on her from above. 'Please, please get me out of this place.'

Although they heard a lot of noises and movement, amazingly and thankfully they had no more fearsome encounters. Eventually they emerged from the forest and found themselves on the foothills of the mountain. There were still a few trees dotted around, but these were poor specimens, obviously having little soil depth. Some trees had been completely broken off, probably the result of large creatures simply careering over them. They walked along the edge of the forest in a southerly direction, taking care to avoid the many obstacles that littered the way, and at the same time watching and listening for any telltale signs of danger. The further they travelled, the more careful they became, as they were aware that they were again nearing the area where the village was situated and human activity was more likely.

Suddenly they heard rhythmic chanting and a drumming noise. They dived back into the trees, waited and watched. After a while, a group of men emerged in something of a line, with the chief leading them. Four of the men were carrying poles with dead creatures hanging from them and others had hollow logs that they were banging with sticks. 'I wonder what that's all about?' whispered Oliver.

'Hmm, I reckon it's some sort of ritual, a sacrifice, but where are they going, I wonder?'

As they watched, the procession suddenly disappeared from view into a depression, a rift in the ground that was out of sight to them.

'Come on,' said Jess. 'I think this might be our opportunity to see what's going on.'

They moved out into the open and looked carefully to their left to make sure that no more people were watching from the trees. They could see no one, so they began to climb the slope parallel to the rift; looking over the edge, they could see that it was a well-worn path – it was obviously a regular ritual. They couldn't see the men, but they could still hear the chanting, so they climbed higher until eventually they could see the men and observe what they were doing. They had stopped by a great slab of rock and were loading the animal carcasses on top. Having done that the chanting began again – it was the same phrase repeatedly.

'Can you understand what they're chanting, Olly? Listen carefully.'

Oliver, in his mind, asked for help to hear the chanting clearly. 'Yes, they're saying, "Hear us, O great ones, receive these our gifts." They're calling to their gods.'

Then the chant changed and this time Jess gave the interpretation: '"Spare now our families and eat now your fill." I wonder what that's all about.'

They didn't have to wait long to find out, because suddenly the men backed down the hill as two massive bear-like creatures approached the carcasses.

'They're just like the creatures we saw in the cave on the other side,' whispered Oliver. 'I bet they've had trouble in the past with them attacking the village and this is the way they attempt to keep trouble at bay.'

'Yeah, I reckon you're right, but, you know, those creatures must live in a similar cave too, so this might well be the golden gate and our way out of this place.'

'Great,' responded Oliver sarcastically. 'That means we have to get past those brutes to do so, and personally that doesn't appeal.'

'Maybe there's a way. Hang on a minute and let's see what they do with their meal.'

Both creatures approached the rock and they growled and snarled at each other as they did so. They grabbed a carcass each and carried them to one side. They settled down and started licking them as many animals do prior to gorging their meal.

'This is it,' whispered Jess. 'Come on.'

Oliver wasn't sure what she was doing, but obediently followed as she climbed still higher up the slope. She peered over the edge from time to time and eventually beckoned him to follow as she carefully slid down into the valley. She pointed up the remaining short distance of the rift, and Oliver could now see what she was pointing to. At some point, the men had obviously attempted to block the cave entrance with a massive wooden gate, a useless exercise against such massive brutes, but the remaining timbers were sun-bleached and now appeared as a golden-yellow colour.

They dashed up the slope to the cave and went inside. How they hoped it was now empty and would stay that way until they'd safely passed through! Once inside the same acrid stench met them and almost made them sick. They extracted their devices and turned them on, the light spread out before them and they swept it around to ensure they were on their own. All appeared to be clear and so they began the trek through to freedom.

Initially the cave was a vast cavern, but after a short distance the roof sloped downwards and the walls closed in. They had not travelled far when they heard noises, not from behind, but from somewhere in front. Their hearts sank: just when they thought it would be a simple walk to freedom, another potential obstacle lay ahead.

'What do you reckon it is?' asked Oliver. 'It's not more of those brutes, is it?'

'No, I don't think it is. Listen!'

They stopped moving and turned an ear towards the sound.

'It's a sort of snuffling, whimpering sound – I reckon they've got youngsters,' said Jess.

Again, they moved slowly and quietly forwards and very soon, two miniatures of the massive creatures outside came into view. They may have been miniature versions, but they were still quite large, about the size of a big St Bernard dog. They almost filled the passage.

'They could still be dangerous, Jess, so how are we going to get past them? I can't see any ledges in this cave, so I don't know what we can do.'

'Hang on a minute, Olly, I've just noticed something – their eyes have not opened yet and although they might hear, feel and smell us, they can't see us. So I say we risk shuffling past them. Are you up for it?'

'Yeah, I don't see any alternative, let's go for it. They look quite cuddly, perhaps they are.'

'I wouldn't bet on it. Anyway, let's go.'

With some trepidation, they began their approach and at that point came that inner voice, 'Be bold and don't fear.' That was just the spur needed and with Jess leading the way, they began to walk past the creatures. The sound from them changed from a whimper to a terrible hissing, but neither beast made a move towards them and it took just a few steps to carry them well clear. It was just in time, it seemed, as one of the adults had heard the hissing and came inside to investigate. It could obviously hear Oliver and Jess retreating up the passage and it gave a mighty roar that echoed all around the cavern and along the tunnel. The cacophony spurred them on, speeding up their pace accordingly.

After about an hour's walk, they began to feel a breeze blowing through and this, they hoped, heralded the exit. They both breathed deeply, attempting to rid themselves of the foul smell that still lingered in their nostrils.

'I never knew fresh air could smell so sweet,' breathed Jess.

Moments later a tiny glimmer of light appeared up ahead. Walking towards the light meant they could see where they were going, so they were able to switch off their devices. The exit was quite tiny and they had to remove their rucksacks to be able to squeeze through. Once through they found themselves in a narrow corridor between high rocks, so they were still unable to see what lay beyond. However, it didn't take them long to negotiate the passageway and they then emerged to a most amazing sight. Before their eyes was the kind of terrain they were used to in England, but beyond the lush grassland before them was a lake whose size was entirely indeterminate, stretching as far as the eye could see in all directions. This confirmed the message they'd received; this was their place of rest for the night, here on the bank of this vast expanse of water. This was a most wonderful and welcome sight, something they again gave thanks for.

11. The Land of Promise

Both Jess and Oliver were desperately tired, hungry and thirsty. They'd had nothing since lunch and their mouths were watering at the thought of what they might have for their evening meal. However, something else ranked far higher for Jess – she wanted to shower, she wanted to wash away all the filth and stench of the day, and she needed a change of clothes. This was in direct contrast to how she had lived on the streets.

It was now early evening and the house should have been visible, but it had not appeared, as far as they could see. Were they again looking in the wrong place, as they had last time, or were they simply missing something? They could see for miles in both directions, but it was nowhere in view. This was rather worrying. They checked their devices under DAY, but it simply said 'rest on the banks of the waters'.

'Surely we're not expected to literally rest on the bank and sleep on the ground overnight? That would be totally unrealistic,' moaned Jess. 'I want a proper meal and a comfortable bed, please. I've had enough of sleeping rough. I assume there are no predators here, though.'

'Hmm, Jess, I wonder if it actually means we're just to sit and rest here for a while and either further directions will come or the house will appear. Do you think that's possible?'

'You could be right I suppose. I guess I was a bit demanding, so lesson learned. Anyway, let's test your theory, let's just sit here and enjoy the scenery for a while. It's been a tough old day and not at all easy to cope with, having to be constantly alert for danger. You're right, Olly; it is good to simply rest and mull over what we've experienced. What do you feel is the most important thing you've learned from the quest?'

'Well... I suppose there are quite a lot of things, but probably it's learning to listen, trust and not to panic when things come my way that are hard to cope with or I don't understand. In that dream, panic made me act the way I did – running away was the only thing I felt able to do. I think if I ever have that dream again, I want to think about stuff first.'

Jess laughed. 'Olly, one thing I've learned is how much you've changed. You really think about stuff and I guess you aren't as scared of everything. For me, the other things I've learned are very similar to what you shared, but you know, I think I appreciate stuff more. I mean, I'm grateful for the good things all around us – sitting here looking out over the water is so peaceful and it's a beautiful scene; in the past I probably wouldn't have noticed such things.'

'What about the thing you most long for, what would that be?'

'Ah, that's easy, family: feeling that I'm loved and wanted and belong. I think you've made me feel that way; I really don't want to be parted from you.'

'Yeah... I truly want my family back together, but it would be great if you were part of it.'

They leaned towards each other and hugged for quite some time. Not for the first time tears flowed down their faces, and they knew their experience to date had forged a bond between them that time would not easily break. What the future held for them they couldn't possibly know, but how they hoped that their closeness would never end. They hugged and Jess suddenly noticed over Oliver's shoulder that the house had now appeared.

'Hey, Olly, do you see what I see?' she said in his ear. Oliver turned his head, and, like Jess, was delighted that they could now go and enjoy a much-needed shower and fabulous evening meal. They jumped to their feet and, grabbing their rucksacks, they moved towards the house, still with an arm around each other.

Later, much refreshed by a shower and a change of clothes, they went through to the kitchen to get the meal of their choice – spaghetti bolognese followed by apple and blackberry crumble for Oliver, and chicken wrapped in ham and smothered with melted cheese, and profiteroles to follow for Jess. After their meal they felt satisfied and at peace with the world. It had been such a hectic day so it was truly great to sit and relax. Silence didn't figure in their evening, though, they had so much to talk about – all that they'd experienced together, but also anticipating what they might experience tomorrow. Later they were really tired and relieved to fall into bed. Jess, just as she had predicted, did dream about creepy-crawlies, but rather than feeling revulsion, as she normally would, she simply brushed them aside – they were no big deal. Later, however, they did both have their usual dream and once again they were standing outside that house; this time the voice said, 'Nearly there, just one more test. Face this challenge head-on.'

Next morning, despite their dreams, they awoke deeply refreshed and raring to go. Today they would face their final test and then it was, they assumed, a straight run to that house and... what? What was it they would experience? Their excitement was mounting. They met before breakfast, with the customary hug, brimming over with real exuberance.

'Well, what do you think today is going to bring, Olly – did you get a message with a dream?'

'Yeah, strange, wasn't it – it's the last test and we're nearly there, but I wasn't sure what was meant by facing the challenge head-on! As I thought about all we'd experienced on other days, I would have said we faced those head-on, so what's the difference this time, I wonder?'

'Hmm, good question. I guess we won't know until we check our devices and see what message we get there. Anyway, let's get some breakfast; I'm sure we'll think better on a full stomach.' With that, Jess led the way into the kitchen.

Their breakfast, in fact, didn't help in their predictions as to what lay ahead, but a hearty meal did increase their desire and determination – they would face whatever came their way and they would succeed. With that, they went and finished preparing and returned equipped to go. As they'd learned to do, they checked the views from the windows, and it was a tremendous relief not to see wild creatures ready to attack them. For the first time on their journeying, the sun was not shining beautifully; it was in fact overcast and the water looked a dull grey. They left the house and noticed that although it was not cold, there was a slight chill to the breeze.

They now consulted their devices. The instructions were brief. 'Cross the water by the shortest route. Use your initiative – face the obstacle head-on. You rest tonight in *that* house.'

'Wow, tonight we get there, that's fantastic!' exclaimed Jess.

'Yeah, that's as maybe, but we still have to get to the other side of the water and I can't see the other side from here – it's vast. So, what do we do? What do you understand by the "shortest route"?'

'I assume there must be a place where the water narrows, or may be shallower, but which direction do we go, right or left?'

Oliver scratched his head and shrugged his shoulders. 'We can't possibly know, so I suggest we walk about a mile one way and then if that doesn't work, we return and go the other way. Mind you, even then that might not be far enough. I just don't know, but we have to try something.'

Jess suddenly had a thought: 'Hey, perhaps there's an inflatable dinghy somewhere in the house. Let's have a look.' They turned around, but the space where the house had stood was now empty; it had vanished. 'That good idea came to nothing, so I guess there wasn't a dinghy there. Come on; let's give your idea a shot.'

They set off, but after what they estimated must have been a good mile, the depth hadn't changed, so they turned back, and having reached their starting point, they set off in the opposite direction, but the outcome was exactly the same.

'Jess, let's sit and think about this for a while; could the instruction have another meaning? It said "face it head-on". What does that suggest to you?'

'Oh no, you're not thinking what I think you're thinking, are you?'

Oliver nodded, 'I rather think so.'

'You have to be joking, cross the water without a boat! How on earth do we do that – sitting on a log?'

'I really don't think so, Jess. I've looked around and I don't think there are any suitable logs around. There's no way I could swim that distance, either. I'm not a strong swimmer.'

'I can hardly swim at all. I reckon I could stay afloat for a while, but that wouldn't get us across to the other side. I think we need help.'

They sat and quietly listened for that inner voice. At first, nothing seemed to be forthcoming, but after a while, the voice spoke: 'Face the obstacle and imagine how you might overcome it; what options come to mind?'

They compared notes and found they had both received the same message. 'What comes to your mind, Olly? I can't get anything that makes sense at the moment.'

Oliver gave a little cough. 'Well... er... what comes to my mind is some things I heard in an RS lesson at school. For instance, there was a guy, I think his name was Moses, and he parted the waters so that people could cross a sea. Then there was Jesus, and He walked on the water. Actually, I think there was someone else who began to walk, but started to sink. I don't think any of those thoughts help us, but I don't have anything else.'

'Doesn't sound very likely, but nothing at all comes to my mind,' Jess responded with a shake of her head. 'I'm totally at a loss.'

They were quiet for a few moments and that inner voice came: 'What are you waiting for?'

'What!' they both exclaimed simultaneously.

'What are we meant to do, part the water or walk on top? Neither seems in the least likely to me,' said Jess.

Oliver lifted his hands in a questioning manner. 'We could try it, I suppose. Do we take our shoes and socks off? I don't fancy a soaking.'

Jess laughed and jumped to her feet. 'Come on, we have nothing to lose.' They both went to the water's edge. 'OK, Olly, you remember the story, what do we do to part the water?'

'I think Moses just pointed his walking stick across the sea and it parted, but neither of us has got a walking stick so we can't do that. I'll try it with my arm.' He lifted his arm parallel to the water and said 'Part!' Nothing happened, so he tried again: 'Part, please!' Again, nothing happened. 'Do you fancy walking?'

Jess shrugged her shoulders, but then together they stepped out and immediately got their feet wet. 'I don't think we quite got it right, Olly. We really do need some clearer instructions.' She shut her eyes. 'Please, tell us what we're meant to do.'

Moments later the voice simply said, 'Do you believe you can do it? Are you prepared to trust Me? Did you try those things believing they would work, or were you certain they wouldn't?'

'Ah, I think I understand,' Oliver responded. 'I certainly didn't think it would work – I didn't trust that it would, but that was because I wasn't certain that it was what we were meant to do.'

'In all truth, I didn't think either would work. I guess I've always been a bit of a sceptic, but over the past days I have come to believe that anything could be possible. Mind you, parting the water and walking on water still feel outside my realm of what's possible.'

'But are we willing to trust now? It seems it's being confirmed that we have got it right, though which, I'm not sure, so can we believe that we can do it?'

'That inner voice has always been right in the past, so yes, I believe we can. Let's go again.'

They climbed to their feet and went back to the water. 'Please help us to believe and trust!' they said. With that, together they stepped out onto the water and this time, to their astonishment and great relief, they stayed on top. They took a few tentative steps and remained on the surface. As they progressed their confidence grew, but even so, both were constantly whispering 'Thank you!' under their breath. They progressed well, but neither dared to talk, as they felt it was essential to stay focused and to concentrate their efforts into completing the challenge. It was still impossible to see the opposite shore and yet that was the sight that they longed for more than anything – water walking was something they were not comfortable doing. It was that distant horizon where they fixed their gaze; they couldn't bring themselves to look down. The sky above them was still steely grey, but ahead blacker clouds were beginning to form. It started to get much darker and a stiff breeze began to blow across the water. They were quite cold now and longed for the ordeal to be over, but the end was nowhere in sight.

Crossing the water was the only way to the house, so turning back was not an option; they just had to press on, no matter how difficult it became, or what the elements might throw at them. They tried to erase from their awareness that there was deep water beneath them: the feeling was not exactly of walking on solid ground, but rather it had a spongy feel, like walking on a trampoline. What concerned them now was the fact that the sky above was getting darker and great storm clouds were sweeping across the sky. It all looked extremely threatening. It didn't remain just a threat for long and very suddenly, a tremendously strong storm-force wind struck them, almost knocking them off their feet. More was to come when freezing cold rain lashed them from head to toe, stinging their faces like thousands of sharp needles. The open water afforded them no place to shelter from the blast; they were extremely exposed and hardly able to move forwards in the face of the storm. They linked arms for mutual support and encouragement and although they bent low, progress was painfully slow.

They battled on for quite some time, but exhaustion was setting in and so they both simultaneously cried, 'Help!'

The inner voice immediately responded, 'Be still! Peace!'

They thought at first it was an instruction to them and so they stopped struggling, but then the wind died down to a whisper and the rain stopped completely. The sky above began to clear as the storm clouds started to slip away. At last, they could again lift their heads, and as they did so, they were amazed to see that the far shore was only a few hundred metres away. Neither could resist a cry of thanks and jubilation – they even risked a hug. So they completed the last short distance in record time; their confidence had grown and their desire to reach their goal ran high.

Moments later, they stepped onto solid ground and turned to look at the obstacle they had just overcome. As if in celebration, the last of the storm clouds drifted away and the sun broke through, bathing the vast waters in brilliant light. It was hard to believe both what they had achieved and what they had experienced, but they had done it – with that hidden helper, they had achieved the impossible.

A quick glance at the time told them that this had taken all morning to accomplish, so it was now time for lunch. A large log was conveniently located on the shore, so that served as their seat as they took out their food packs.

'I must say,' Jess, said with feeling, 'I wish we could get out of our soaking wet clothes, it's not in the least comfortable sitting with clothing clinging all over.'

'Yes,' Oliver responded, 'but the trouble is, we're stuck with them for the rest of the day, because we don't get our usual house again. Next time we're indoors it will be in *that* house. I suppose the sun will dry us a bit, but that's going to take some time.'

'Hmm, too long for my liking, I'm really uncomfortable. Anyway, let's have lunch and see how we feel afterwards.'

Lunch tasted truly great; they hadn't realised just how hungry and thirsty they were. The food gave them renewed strength, a fresh resolve. The sun was now very hot and all cloud cover had disappeared; they were beginning to dry off, but their clothes still chafed their legs.

'Jess, I think I'm going to have to remove my outer clothes and hang them on the bushes to dry. I reckon if the air could circulate around them, they'd soon be OK to wear. I promise not to look in your direction if you want to do the same.'

Jess agreed it was a good suggestion, so they slipped off their outer clothes and hung them on a bush in the full sun and almost immediately, steam began to rise from them. They sat with the bush between them and waited for everything to dry. They were aware that they didn't know how much ground they still had to cover, so didn't want to delay too long. Oliver consulted his device for any updates and found there was in fact a new message. It read, 'Congratulations! You're nearly there. Just walk and trust; your footsteps will be guided.'

He shared his discovery with Jess. 'Hey Jess, have you looked at your device recently?' He read the message to her. 'What do you think?'

'I suppose "just walk" means exactly that – basically, we'll get there when we get there. So, do you think we're back in England? Try that mobile again, Olly.'

Oliver searched his rucksack and located Jez's mobile; he switched it on and although it was still showing fully charged, there was no signal. 'No, nothing,' he responded. 'Maybe we won't get back properly till after we've visited that house for real.'

Oliver jumped to his feet and went to the front of the bush to check his clothes. The drying was going well, so he turned them over and then went and sat down again.

'How are they doing?' asked Jess. 'Anywhere near dry?'

'Getting there,' he responded. 'How about yours?'

'Yeah, another few minutes and I reckon they'll be OK. I don't know about you, but I'm keen to get going, because I want to see that house for real – I reckon it holds some answers and I want to know what those answers are. I'm hoping it will tell me who I really am, where I've come from and where I'm going – and I just hope I like what I hear.'

After another half hour, everything was dry enough to wear, so they redressed and made ready to move out on the final leg of their epic journey.

12. A Divine Encounter

'Which way do we go now?' questioned Oliver. 'Do you think it's still westerly? It did say our steps would be guided, so maybe it doesn't really matter in which direction we start off, as we'll always finish in the right place.'

'It's been westerly all along,' answered Jess, 'so let's continue that way. I'm sure you're right that it doesn't really matter, so we'll just see where our feet take us.'

The shore of the lake was lower than the surrounding area, so when they reached the higher ground they had a lovely panoramic view of the countryside beyond. It was beautiful: green and sort of familiar. This was such a contrast to the prehistoric land they had just left behind – this looked more like England. There was no obvious path ahead, no well-worn tracks, nothing to determine where they should walk. Strangely, there were no hedges or walls, so no clues to indicate where they were. There were trees dotted around and they appeared to be familiar species; also, they could see what looked like a small wood in the distance, but no buildings of any description.

They set off with the wooded area as their target. There was a spring in their step as they excitedly anticipated what lay ahead, but how soon they would locate that house was impossible to know. However, one thing they knew for certain was that it would be today, and there were not many hours left before night. They walked and talked and the miles passed quickly. It was strange that everywhere was grassy and seemed to have no undulations, no rocks and no obstacles whatsoever. It did make walking easier, but suddenly they realised that none of the trees ever got nearer and the wooded area seemed to move to their right.

'Our direction has been adjusted Jess, have you noticed? But it's very strange that we never get any closer to any of the trees. This is like walking in a dream, except that in dreams, walking sometimes feels like wading through treacle. I really don't understand what's going on here; why can't we just go straight to that house and get on with getting answers?'

'Well, let's face it Olly, nothing about this quest has been "normal" and some things have been extremely weird. The point is, of course, that although we reach that house today, we might not get any answers straight away. I think we will have to spend the night there first.'

'Yeah, that's a point, Jess. I hadn't thought about it like that. Hmm, a bit longer to wait. I wonder if we get everything provided in that house as we have in the other house, or do we have to use our food packs?'

'Well, for just one more night I think I could live with the food pack, but generosity has marked our whole journey, so who knows what that house will come up with? I'm focusing on the ultimate, Olly – tomorrow is where I want us to get to, so the in-between is just a means to an end.'

They continued to walk for the rest of the afternoon, and they noticed that the landmark trees always remained at a similar distance from them. Even more strangely, although they from time to time changed direction, the landmarks remained in the same relationship to them. It was late afternoon when at last the first building they'd seen that day appeared on the horizon. Would it, like everything else, fail to get any closer? In fact, this time it did get closer, and, as they progressed, they began to hope that this was their ultimate destination.

'Jess, does that building look vaguely familiar to you?'

'You know, I think it might. There's something about it that I reckon I've seen before, but as it's always been in dreams, I can't be sure yet – and I think we're seeing it from the side instead of from the front, as we've normally seen it.'

It was not long till they reached the house, and viewing it from the front brought confirmation – it was the same house they had both seen in so many of their dreams. In the dreams they had been inside, of course, but every time, they had been in a bedroom, so had never even glimpsed the other rooms. Even though they had always bolted down the stairs and through the door at the bottom, they had never seen the room they had rushed into (a lounge area), because they always woke up at that precise moment. They stood looking at the house for quite some time and eventually walked all around it, always staying at a distance of about twenty metres. There was no garden and no fences; the house was simply set on the grassy land. What were they about to experience? Was anyone in the house, would it hold terrifying memories?

They knew they had to approach the house; their destiny, it seemed, depended on them doing so.

'Are you up for this, then, Jess – shall we go and see if anyone's at home?'

'Absolutely, I'm more than ready. Anyway, anything beats sleeping rough, and I've slept in some terrible dumps over the years, so let's go for it.'

Together they walked to the front door and, very hesitatingly, knocked. They waited a while but no one came so they knocked again, harder and louder this time. There was no response so they tentatively opened the door and shouted, but again there was no reply. They went inside and began to look around. The door had opened into a small hallway with a cloakroom to the right and a lounge to the left. Straight ahead was the staircase – which looked very familiar. Beyond the lounge was a dining room, and to the right of the dining room was the kitchen. There was no sign of life, but the table had place settings for two diners. They felt the urge to explore upstairs, so retraced their steps to the hallway. They ascended the stairs, looking and listening as they did so, as they were uncertain as to whether they would encounter something from their dreams. Upstairs there were three bedrooms and a bathroom, and both Oliver and Jess recognised the rooms that featured in their dreams – nothing had changed. The third room was obviously for a couple, as it had two single beds and a large wardrobe. Were other guests expected?

'It's weird seeing our rooms in daylight,' Jess remarked, 'and did you notice, all our things are here, nightwear, clean clothing and toiletries. It is obviously a different house from the one we've used on our travels, but this one appears to supply all our needs just the same.'

'You're right, I hadn't noticed our things, but I'm glad everything is here for us: it's most definitely time for a change of clothes after our drenching! I suggest we shower, change, then go and try out the kitchen. I have to admit that I am feeling rather hungry. It seems a long time since we had lunch.'

They both opted to shower and change before dinner, and the feel of lovely warm water caressing their skin was a wonderfully refreshing experience. They had to take it in turns in this house, because unlike the other house this one did not have en suite facilities. It didn't take either of them long to dress, and then they descended to the kitchen. Walking down the stairs was somewhat emotional, as their thoughts immediately turned to their nightmare experiences.

'How did you feel on the stairs?' asked Jess.

'Not good,' Oliver replied. 'It brought back horrible memories – I almost had to rush to get through the door at the bottom, but I feel OK now. How about you?'

'Yeah, just like you said. I really hope those feelings of dread will be dealt with by the end of this visit. Do you have a feeling you know this house from somewhere – I don't mean from our dreams, but a real house that you've visited at some point in the distant past?'

'Yes! But I thought it was just my memory playing tricks on me, because of the dreams. So where do you think we might have seen it before? Isn't it odd that we should feel the same! I'm sure we've not been in a similar house together since we met, but how can it have been before we met?'

'Hmm, it's another of those weird coincidences that keep cropping up, but maybe that's another thing that'll be sorted out while we're here – I hope so, anyway.'

Their thoughts turned to dinner and this time their choices were the same, a roast chicken dinner with all the trimmings, followed by apple and blackberry crumble and custard. Once again, it was a sumptuous meal and afterwards they cleared everything away before settling down for a relaxing evening. They put music on Jess' device to play in the background, music that was especially soothing and yet at the same time lifted their spirits. They talked openly and freely, eagerly anticipating what tomorrow would bring, and although they were exhilarated by the thought that their quest would reach its conclusion, something of a nervousness still lingered – what if they didn't entirely welcome the outcome; what if they were parted and sent off in opposite directions? That latter thought was altogether too horrible to contemplate; surely, having brought them together, no one would be so cruel as to force them apart again? However, past experiences told them that in reality people could be very cruel and uncaring. But not Gabriel – he was not like that. Gabriel was exceptional, always seeking the best for everyone, so they had confidence that what lay ahead would be the best for them. They consoled themselves with that thought.

During one lull in their conversation, Oliver suddenly had a memory flashback. 'Jess, something has just come to me. This house is just like my grandma's house. I think that's why it looks familiar – even the carpet on the stairs is like the one she had. That doesn't explain *your* feelings, though, unless you visited a similar house somewhere. Can you recall anywhere you've been that fits with this house?'

'I don't think so, though I can't be sure of that. I think there is something in my deepest memory that holds the clue, but I just can't reach it. Maybe it will surface at some point, but right now, the more I probe the deeper it seems to go.'

It was getting quite late and they realised that they really ought to be going to bed. Both were somewhat reluctant to do so, as this might be their last night together and they wanted to make it last as long as they could. There was also another reason for their disinclination – the fear of nightmares; after all, this was *that* house and to date that was what it meant for them, but their hope was that tonight would be different. It was with great reluctance that they went upstairs, and with a final hug on the landing, they went into their rooms and got ready for bed.

Although they were both extremely tired, sleep did not come easily, as they were too keyed up inside. Unknown to each other, they simultaneously turned their devices to MUS and allowed the soothing sounds to flow over them and into their troubled minds. The effect was almost instantaneous as their jumbled thoughts began to ebb away and a deep sense of peace descended. Both were quickly lulled into deep, refreshing sleep.

However, a few hours later, the dreams began. As always, they were in bed in their rooms (where in fact they now were) when, in their dreams, a terrible apprehension descended on them, the feeling that something or someone was drawing close. Fear gripped their hearts and the inclination to run welled up within and caused them to jump out of bed and rush for the door and the stairs. They were entirely unaware of each other, although both of them together were fleeing for their lives. The presence, whatever it was, they sensed was bearing down on them and they rushed down the stairs seemingly touching none of the steps. They reached the bottom but were unable to escape through the door to their right.

A voice spoke; a most gentle, beautiful and calming voice – it was the same voice, that 'inner voice' they had been listening to during their journeying: 'Calm your fears, Jess, and you, too, Oliver. Why are you frightened, why are you running from Me? I have never wished to hurt you: did not My servants whom I sent to you reassure you that My plan is to provide the best for you, to give you hope and a blessed future? As you now stand at that door, I am standing at the door of your life. My desire is to come in and then I can direct your future pathway. Will you let Me in? Will you accept My love and will you allow Me to provide the best for you for the rest of your lives?'

Both of them were now fully awake and realised this was all happening for real. Oliver opened the door to the lounge area and he and Jess walked in, and then the most fantastically bright light filled the room as the presence they had felt followed them into the room. Jess and Oliver involuntarily fell to their knees with their heads bowed. Both felt a hand touch their heads and that familiar gentle electric shock-like feeling surged throughout their bodies, but at the same time, they felt a deep sense of calm fall on them. Love for that 'presence' welled up within them and they knew this was the beginning of something, a 'relationship' that was truly beautiful and was forever. Tears flowed freely down their cheeks – not fear, not regret, but thankfulness and joy.

Then the light faded and was gone; after a while, Jess and Oliver climbed to their feet and immediately hugged each other for quite some time. They knew something special had just happened to them; they were different, and in future everything would be different – purposeful and exciting. What were they supposed to do now?

When Oliver looked at his watch, he was amazed to find that it was eight o'clock. It was morning – a special morning they'd long anticipated, so what would today bring and how would it fit with what they'd just experienced? They went back upstairs to dress and prepare for the day, intending to come down, have breakfast and wait and see what happened next. The stairs, they both found, now held no bad memories for them. The nightmares, they knew for sure, were gone forever – this was a new beginning. They were free from the past.

A while later they met on the landing and went downstairs together, but when they opened the door to enter the lounge they were amazed to find they were no longer alone. Three people were there to greet them – Marianne, Joshua and Gabriel. Oliver just didn't know who to go to first, but the three solved the problem for him by forming a group hug that included Jess. Afterwards Oliver introduced her to Marianne and Joshua, and for quite some time they talked together. It was an extremely animated Jess and Oliver who shared their experiences.

'I understand you have met our Father,' said Joshua. 'How did you find the experience?'

'Your Father?' questioned Jess. 'When did we meet your Father?'

'Just a short time ago,' he responded with a laugh. 'When you came downstairs after your dream, it was He who spoke to you and laid His hands on you – did you feel His presence?'

'Wow!' exclaimed Oliver. 'That was your Father? But why could we only see a bright light? Yes, we felt His touch; it was beautiful, electrifying – I felt as though something had changed inside me. I feel as though I'm not the same person any more. Can you explain what it was all about?'

'That's what we're here for,' Marianne answered. 'You're right, though, you are not the same person any more. You've taken a very significant step, but there is so much more that your Heavenly Father wants for you both. Most of all He wants a relationship where not only does He know and love you, but you know and love Him. That became possible when Jesus, His most wonderful Son, came to earth to die on the cross to save the world – to save you and help you begin a new life. Have you heard of Jesus and exactly what He did?'

'Yes, yes I think I'm beginning to understand,' Oliver responded. 'Didn't He come at Christmas and die at Easter? Is that what you mean? We were told that at Sunday school.'

'Yeah, that rings a bell with me,' said Jess, 'but I've never really understood what it means for us. Why did He come and why did He have to die – couldn't He just have told people what was expected of them?'

'Actually, Jess,' said Gabriel picking up from Marianne, 'our Heavenly Father, who is also your Heavenly Father, tried that in the past, but no one could achieve what was required of them. Nobody, by their own efforts, is good enough to live in relationship with a holy God, but He doesn't want to exclude anyone from His presence, so that's why Jesus came. His death paid the price for all that's wrong in people's lives, so now when anyone accepts that they need Jesus' gift and they welcome Him into their lives, everything changes – they can enjoy a wonderful future with Jesus to guide them by His Holy Spirit. We know that your experiences of fatherhood have not been good in the past, but our Heavenly Father is everything that you could ever have wished from an earthly father, and so much more.'

Joshua again spoke: 'You said you felt His electrifying touch and you felt something had changed within you. Well, that was the point at which He gave you the first part of His best gift to you – He gave you a first touch of His Spirit. There's more to come if you are willing to receive it by surrendering your life and your will to Him. Let Him permanently live in you and through you – it would be a decision you would never regret. The benefits are not just for the present but also forever and ever. You, like us, will dwell in His presence always. One day your body will die, but your spirit will live in His presence for eternity. It is a fantastic place to be – we know, because that's our real home.'

'Yeah, I think I understand now. So what do we need to do? Because whatever it is, I'm up for it!' said Jess enthusiastically.

Oliver could hardly speak because tears were flowing down his cheeks. Jess flung her arms around him and they clung together for some time. Eventually he was able to speak between sobs: 'I don't... ever remember being... loved that much and I just want that relationship with... is it with Jesus or the Father?'

'It's both,' answered Marianne gently. 'They are truly one together with the Holy Spirit. So all you have to do is pray; we can lead you, so is that what you want?'

They both acknowledged that it was what they wanted, so they all knelt on the floor and Marianne spoke the words for them to repeat:

'Father God, thank You for the tremendous love You have shown towards all people in allowing Jesus to die for us. I acknowledge that I have so far lived my life far from You and without giving You a thought. Please forgive me, change me and help me from now onwards to live my life Your way. Live in me by the power of Your Holy Spirit and help me now to grow more and more like You each day. Help me to trust You for the future and for eternity. Amen.'

After the prayer, the three guides laid their hands on them and Jess and Oliver experienced once more a tremendous surge of power pass through them. They felt a tremendous exhilaration – a joy such as they'd never felt before.

The three helped Jess and Oliver to their feet and they all embraced. 'Welcome to your Father's family,' said Gabriel. 'May His love, joy and presence fill you daily, as you live your life with Him and for Him. He's now given you His Spirit to help you, and He will guide you and help you always if you call upon Him.' He gave them both a

Bible of their own. 'Read this,' said Gabriel. 'This contains the Father's teaching for humankind. Let it always guide you through life. You'll find it has two parts to it; begin with the second part, it's called the New Testament, and it will help you become established. You will also need the support of others, so we would encourage you to go to the church which has been chosen for you to become part of.'

'Now, I am aware that you have not yet eaten today,' said Joshua, 'so let's go through to the dining room and have breakfast.'

They went through and they all sat at the table, but then Gabriel elected to serve them. They made their choices and in double quick time the food arrived – this time Marianne, Joshua and Gabriel ate with them.

'You're eating with us today,' Oliver remarked. 'That's nice – only Gabriel has done that in the past.'

'That's true, I haven't eaten with you in the past,' Marianne answered with a smile, 'but today's special, it's your re-birthday and is to be a day of great celebration. More will come later, but this is the start. It's also the opportunity for you to ask questions, as I'm sure there's much you want to know.'

How right she was: question after question tumbled out and Jess set the ball rolling. 'Why were we sent on this quest, and why is this house so important?'

Joshua paused for a few moments before answering. 'Before it all began, both of you, entirely separately, were becoming more and more miserable, you had lost your self-worth and your lives lacked any hope of things ever changing. Fear can either paralyse people or make them behave irrationally. Both of you were showing such

189

behavioural traits. The quest, as you call it, was initially to draw you both together and to set you on a path where you would discover yourselves afresh and become emotionally stronger – you have faced some tough tests, but together you have overcome. Your being together is all part of a bigger picture that is yet to be revealed. This house and the dreams you both had were a means to an end: both of you, as in the dreams, were running away, frightened of the truth, frightened of the future and unable to listen. Listening to that inner voice, which incidentally was the Father's voice, has been an important part of the tests you have undertaken. And now you've taken that most important step. Also, you have received the Father's gift and you are ready to face the world. In your relationship with the Father you are strong and all things become possible. Believe and trust Him always.'

'Let's go back to the lounge now,' suggested Gabriel. 'We'll be comfortable there and you can continue to ask your questions. Incidentally, this house is also important for others, but more about that later.'

13. Revelation

The questions and answers continued to flow. Throughout this time, Oliver and Jess were learning more about themselves and each other, as well as insights into spiritual matters – their inquisitive minds working overtime. Their three guides explained something of what it meant to be given a new start, new hope, and how their lives might develop from now onwards. They explained about the Church, how the intention was that it would be the body of Jesus on earth and its role would be to share the good news with others. Walking the path of faith, Joshua warned them, would not always be easy and they could suffer much for their stance, but they would never be alone and would never regret their decision.

Later they went out into the fresh air and gazing at the view before them, remembered how the landmarks never got any closer. Oliver eventually spoke out about it: 'Why is it that the landmarks, such as those trees, never got any closer?'

'We thought you might wonder about that,' laughed Marianne, 'but in fact this landscape is not real; it just appears to be.'

'So everything we've seen and experienced was unreal; just a sort of dream?'

'Oh, no, not a dream: it has all been very real, but it has all been specially created by your Heavenly Father to present you with a challenge and so build your confidence – to prove how strong you are deep down. You had lost your confidence and self-worth and you needed to have that confidence and self-worth restored. The bygone age, for instance, doesn't actually exist in today's world, but everything was genuine – the animals you encountered were savage and dangerous; you haven't been duped in any way; that wouldn't have been honest. Remember this: you really did walk on water and could have sunk into the depths if you had doubted. The house you stayed in each night was obviously real, as is this house, the subject of your dreams. We have never been and will never be dishonest in our dealings with you. Remember, though, you are stronger now than you ever were in the past – in future He will be with you and enable you to do what is best. He will strengthen you whenever difficulties arise.'

Time passed extremely quickly and Gabriel suddenly announced that it was lunchtime and they needed to go back indoors. 'There are people we want you to meet, so you may want to go to your rooms to prepare for what I feel sure will be a great surprise, but will bring great delight to you both. It's time for that final chapter. When you're ready, come down and one of us will take you through.'

Jess and Oliver went up to their rooms, but were not there long and both returned within moments of each other, anxious to know what surprises were in store for them this time.

It was a 'butterflies in the stomach moment' and both were excited and nervous at the same time, but they did want to open that final chapter and see what the final page had to tell them.

Marianne met them and embraced them. 'Be calm, there's no need for you to fear in the least,' she whispered. Once again, as Oliver had experienced in the past, that sense of well-being descended on them. Marianne approached the door to the dining room and turned the handle; she opened the door and beckoned them inside. The first thing they noticed was that the table was laden with a fantastic array of food; it was indeed a banquet. That in itself was a lovely sight, but they'd expected something else and Joshua could see the look of disappointment on their faces.

'I can see that you expected more, and more is to come, so don't be downhearted. What in fact is your heart's desire – what would be the best thing you could imagine?'

Oliver spoke first.

'No contest for me, I want my family to get back together and be happy, but I want Jess to be in the picture too.'

'Olly took the words out of my mouth; I can't imagine it being possible, but that's exactly what I want and Olly has to be part of it too. Sorry if we're asking for the impossible.'

'With the Father, nothing is impossible,' responded Gabriel, 'and you were both promised good things at the end of the quest. So let's meet some more guests, shall we?'

As he spoke, he opened the lounge door and a very attractive woman walked in. Oliver did a double take. 'Mum? Is it really you? You look so... so different, younger and happier.' He dived in her direction and embraced her warmly: tears streamed down both their faces and it was some time until they could let go and speak.

He set out to introduce Jess. 'Mum, this is...' He got no further, because his mum rushed forward and embraced Jess.

'Jess? My darling Jess, is it really you? I thought I'd never see you again, you look wonderful, beautiful and... Oh, Jess, this is truly marvellous, you two have fulfilled my wildest dreams! We're back together at last – I just never believed it could happen. It was so awful when we were parted – I'm so sorry for what you had to put up with!'

'M... Mum!' stuttered Jess. 'But if you're Olly's mum too, that means...'

'Yes, my darlings, you and Oliver are brother and sister.'

'My sister! Jess, you really are my sister – I always thought my pretend sister had been real, once! That's absolutely fantastic.'

'And I knew I had a brother called Olly! With everything I've been through, I must have blocked it out!' cried Jess.

They grabbed each other and danced around the room – the unbelievable had actually happened.

'But how do you both know each other?' questioned their mum incredulously.

'We met in a squat,' Oliver replied. 'Gabriel introduced us and he sent us off on a challenging journey together; you'll never believe what we've seen, what we've done and how we've changed.'

'I am so sorry, my darlings, that you had to face such terrible ordeals...' Their mum's voice was hoarse with emotion. 'I was in such a deep, dark place, but it's no excuse for neglecting you both and allowing those horrible men to treat you as they did. Can you possibly forgive me?'

Neither answered with words, but both rushed to embrace her and their tears flowed freely

'So how come you're here in this house, did someone invite you?' asked Oliver.

'You could say that. Before I answer that, let me ask you a question – have you two been having dreams about this house?'

'Yes, we have,' answered Jess, 'but why do you ask?'

'Well, that's why I'm here. I dreamed too and I was sent off to meet this beautiful lady. She said I had to find this house and all would be resolved. Great joy would fill my heart. I too have been on a long voyage of discovery, I've been to some strange places and I met Joshua and Gabriel too. I have learned a lot about myself and recognised many ways I've made a mess of things in the past – I've not protected my family whom I love so very dearly, and everything I hold dear I've practically destroyed. I am so sorry, you two, but if you will give me another chance, I promise I will do my best never to hurt you again. I too have changed and I've begun a new life – Gabriel helped me to see my deepest need and then to do something about it. The Heavenly Father has become my Father.'

Jess and Oliver both hugged their mum again and shed yet more tears – tears of great joy.

'Mum,' said Jess, 'no more blame games – OK? Let's put the past behind us and make a new start together – what do you say, Olly?'

'Yes, I'll second that. We both need you Mum.'

'That's great,' Marianne responded, 'and we're absolutely delighted to hear your resolve: yes, of course there will be some difficult times ahead and many things you will need to work through, but you will now have help to resolve the things of the past. You are stronger now, you will battle through *together* and you will always have help at hand to work through the hurts and pains, even feelings of anger about the past. Your Heavenly Father gave you His greatest gift of all – His Spirit now lives in you and He will lead you into victory.'

'Incidentally, you will have another helper,' Gabriel now spoke. 'Someone else will be standing with you. Just give me a moment.' He went to the door, opened it and beckoned to someone in the room beyond. All eyes turned to the door, wondering who it was that Gabriel was calling. There were great intakes of breath as a man entered the room. Jenny's eyes and mouth opened wide.

'Peter! I don't believe it, is it really you? Wow, wow, wow! This is absolutely fantastic! Are you really coming home? Are we really going to be a family again, are we going to make a new start?'

'I most certainly want to come home if you will let me, my darling Jenny, and I want to ask you all to forgive me for leaving you as I did; it wasn't fair on you and you really didn't deserve it. It was a terrible thing to do – cowardly – I feel disgusted with myself.'

'Oh, Peter, I'm certainly willing to forgive you. I think I did understand it in part – I was always angry with you and I blamed you for so many of our troubles. I said some awful things to you, so I want you to forgive me for the hurt I caused you too.'

Yet more hugs and tears were proof enough that their feelings and desires were genuine; they were back together and the bond between them had the potential to be stronger than ever.

'Hey, you two, don't forget us!' Jess broke in.

'Oh my lovely, lovely children,' Jenny responded, 'you are most certainly part of the wonderful reunion. It couldn't be complete without you. I am so sorry that I or we let you down when you most needed love and support. Can you both forgive us?'

'We'll try, we really will!' said Oliver. 'You getting back together is what I've longed for, so that will really help – and I'm sure Jess feels the same. We'll get there!'

'We've all got a lot of catching up to do; a lot of things to work through,' Peter said. 'I rather think it's going to be tough at times: there will no doubt be tears along the way, but we've all made very important decisions – these three have helped us all to get to know the Father's perfect love, so I've no doubt that He will help us work things through.'

'Er, am I right in thinking that we've all dreamed about this house and had fantastic and strange journeys?' asked Oliver.

It transpired that that was exactly what the whole family had experienced. Marianne, Joshua and Gabriel were instruments that featured in the lives of all. Gabriel went on to explain how the Father's desire and purpose had been to restore their lives and relationships. Ultimately, this family unit was extremely important in His plan and they were all destined to achieve great things in His service.

'How right Mum is. We both need your forgiveness for the pain and hurt and rejection you must have felt: we were selfish in not realising what we were doing to you. I had no idea that you had been taken into care, Jess. I got a job in America and just cut myself off, so presumably no one could find me. I should have returned long ago, but I was so ashamed and felt so unworthy that I couldn't bring myself to attempt a reconciliation – I really didn't think you'd have me back, Jen. Can you forgive me for leaving you in the lurch?'

'I admit I was angry and very bitter at first, Peter, so I'd have given you a hard time – but, darling, I was ill! I became totally dependent on men who wormed their way into my life and our home. Not one of them was a substitute for you and I hated them, I hated myself and I hated what I'd become and was allowing to happen to you two, Jess and Oliver. The journey I've been on has changed me completely – built my self-worth, rooted out all anger and bitterness and given me a new vision for life. A new start? No, more than that, a new life.'

'That just goes to show, not everything has been bad, has it?' suggested Oliver. 'We wouldn't have met these three amazing people if it all hadn't happened, and they've taught us so much and led us to the start of a most wonderful future. So thank you for all you've made possible.'

'Thank you, Oliver, for your kind words,' said Joshua, 'but it has been our privilege and delight to work with you all and to see you wonderfully transformed and reunited, but the real thanks should go to your Heavenly Father. He was the One who initiated everything and it was His plan that we were unfolding for all of you. Love truly conquers everything when the Father is at the helm. It was love that took Jesus to the cross, it was love that kept Him there, but it was love that eventually raised Him from death and that love is the saving grace for all who will believe and trust in Him.'

Gabriel now interrupted: 'I have no doubt that there is much more that you all want to say and no doubt many questions you still need to ask, but may I suggest that it is done over lunch? Your Heavenly Father has ordered this banquet to celebrate the fact that all of you have joined His family, but it is also to celebrate the fact that you are wonderfully reconciled as a family unit – that brings Him, and us, great delight. So let's celebrate, but before we eat, let's give the Father our grateful thanks.'

He led them in a simple prayer of thanksgiving and they all sat down. There was a fantastic variety of cold food on the table and they all helped themselves to the sumptuous fare available. It was the most amiable time imaginable as they all chatted freely and openly. This was a family gathering such as they had never known before. Jess and Oliver had never experienced true peace and happiness in their lives, but now they felt drawn to each other and to their parents in a bond they just knew would never be broken – theirs was a joy unlimited.

After some considerable time, Oliver asked the inevitable question: 'What happens next? I don't suppose we stay here, but do we simply go back to our old home, the one we left behind?'

Marianne stepped in to supply the answer: 'Today and tonight you will stay here, but a new beginning awaits you all – a new home, a new area, a new school, and for you, Peter, a new job. The old has gone, and new things have come. You all needed to be changed from within, if we'd simply sent you back to all you knew previously, everything would quickly have fallen apart again – you would have been robbed of all that the Father wants for you. Now you will have a new future with lives that have been changed. We are unable to give you specific details, but just like the quests you have all been on, you must trust and believe that all will be very, very good, because the Father has your best interests at heart.'

'Now we're going to leave you on your own for the rest of the afternoon. You must have much to talk about and some fresh bonding to do,' said Joshua. 'Feel free to either stay in the house or to walk out in the fresh air.'

They chose to go outside and walked for a while, but then decided to sit on the grass and open their hearts to each other.

Oliver was first to speak. 'Dad, why did you leave when you did? Was it for someone else?'

'No, Oliver, it wasn't anything like that; the problem was that my work was very demanding and I foolishly gave it absolute priority, and as a consequence I neglected the most important people in my life – my family. Mum was going through a difficult patch at that time, but I was never there for her and she got more and more depressed and we began to drift apart. We argued constantly and eventually I decided to move out and focus on my career. Just months later the company closed and it was then that I realised what a fool I'd been, but I was too proud and too stubborn to get in touch with Mum and ask her to forgive me.'

'The bad patch that Dad referred to,' Jenny joined in, 'was postnatal depression; I lost another baby we were expecting, I got to thirty weeks and then everything went pear-shaped. I didn't just lose the baby – other complications meant that I couldn't have any more children and that sent me into the doldrums – I had a nervous breakdown. I said some very cruel and unkind things to Dad – I just lashed out at him, so he was not entirely to blame.'

'I didn't know any of that,' said Oliver, 'It must have been an awful time for you, Mum. Are you OK now?'

'Well, yes, I'm finally getting there, thanks to the timely intervention of Marianne. Part of the problem was that I was being prescribed stronger and stronger drugs for my depression and I was no longer in control of my life. I think I was heading for total disaster. You know, Oliver, how bad things were in our house – well, you saw it too, Jess, just before you were taken into care. All those horrible men in my life; they saw my vulnerability and took advantage. I took advantage of them too I suppose, as they provided some income. You'll remember that none of them stayed long, though. The one who stayed longest was Jez, and he only stayed because he was using the house for drugs and all sorts of stolen goods. He scared me, but I was too weak to do anything about it, and I hated the way he treated you, Oliver. I could see you hurting so much, but he wouldn't allow me to comfort you. And then you ran away. Well, even for me that was a step too far, so I rang the police. When the police finally cornered him he lashed out with a knife so he's where he belongs and hopefully for a long, long time.'

'What happened to you, Jess?' her dad asked.

'I had blotted much of it out, but I remember now. It's just come back to me what happened. One of those horrible men, Arty, I think his name was, he came into my room one night... I can't remember how I got away, but I did, and I locked myself in the bathroom. I was only six at the time, but next morning I was so upset that I told a teacher at the school what had happened and she reported it to a social worker. They took me into care. It wasn't what I wanted, because I didn't believe it was Mum's fault and I desperately missed her and cried for days. Eventually, though, I was fostered by a Mr and Mrs Patterson, but it wasn't a happy home, so when I was eight I ran away and lived as best I could for quite some time, stealing to eat and sleeping wherever I could find shelter.

'Then one day a woman from a church found me and took me to her home. I gave a false name and address so that she couldn't send me back to the Pattersons' house. She was very kind, but then she talked about me having to go to school and I decided no way, and ran away again. I'd only been there for few days.

'Since then I've lived in squats all over and begged to get money for food. I've met a few creeps, but then I met a wonderful man who cared – Gabriel! He was great with all of us. Then I met my lovely brother, Olly, though I didn't know he was really my brother at that point, but we thought of each other as brother and sister!'

'Oh, Jess,' exclaimed Peter. 'If only I'd known, if only I'd bothered to get in touch with you all… I let you down and now I intend to put right some of those wrongs.'

'I never could understand why the police couldn't locate you, Jess,' said Jenny. 'Surely someone reported you missing – why didn't they contact me to see if you'd returned home?'

'I guess the Pattersons would have reported me missing,' responded Jess, 'but I don't know why they didn't see if I'd returned home. I can understand why they never found me, though; there's a vast network of rough sleepers and squats – anyone who doesn't want to be found can basically hide forever. Still, Olly found me and it seems *someone* was watching over me the whole time.'

'Tell us about your incredible journey,' Jenny said, wiping away the tears from her eyes.

Jess and Oliver shared their experiences with their mum and dad, and the more they shared the more their parents' eyes widened, marvelling at their resilience. Some aspects of their stories caused great intakes of breath and looks of incredulity.

'I am so proud of you, my darlings,' Jenny remarked. 'I can't believe you managed to face all that you did, but it does explain why you are both so mature and well-rounded. The crowning glory of it all is the faith you now have and we share with you – it is truly wonderful. If only we'd shared such a faith right from the start, I'm certain it would have cemented us all together.'

'That's true, my love, but I think we've all got a fantastic future ahead of us and all that we've learned on our journeys will prove to be a tremendously strong foundation,' added Peter.

'What job do you think you will have, Dad?' asked Oliver. 'You said the company you worked for closed, but then you said you got another job in America. Did you just leave it, or will you have to hand in your notice?'

'Yes, it was a similar job to the one I'd been doing. But I realised the damage it was doing to my life and, indeed, my health, so I handed in my resignation and started looking for another post back in the UK, one that didn't demand body and soul. I don't know what job I will have next, but I'm sure those three wonderful beings know what's best for me. They are messengers from the Father and that means everything to me. I never believed in angels until I met those three, but now I have no doubt. I really thank them for all the help they've given me, but not only me, but all of you too, my lovely family. You are so precious to me.'

As he spoke he was not ashamed of the tears that began to trickle down his cheeks, but they were the trigger that brought all his family rushing towards him. Never in their lives before had they experienced such a feeling of being one together. After all the trauma they had gone through in the past, this was a very precious moment and one they were determined they would do all in their power to hang on to in the future. With the Father's precious gift flowing within them they knew they had the glue that would hold them together through thick and thin.

They walked and talked for the rest of the afternoon and after yet another sumptuous meal, served by Marianne, Joshua and Gabriel, they continued to talk well into the evening. Time flew by and it was quite late when they suddenly realised how tired they were and decided to go to bed.

'I've slept in this house before,' confided Jenny, 'and I rather suspect your dad has too – am I right, Peter?'

'You most certainly are, but I didn't know that any of you used it also. I rather think some incredible things have been going on without us realising it. I never believed that the spiritual world could be so wonderful. I always imagined it to be dull, boring and irrelevant. Now I'm convinced it's lively, exciting and far from boring. I just want to experience so much more of it!'

With that, they made for the stairs.

'Wait just a moment,' Gabriel interrupted. 'We have to say goodbye to you now; our job is done for the present, so we'll not see you in the morning.'

Oliver ran to Marianne. 'I don't want you to leave,' he said, tearfully. 'We've had such fantastic times together and I don't want it to end.'

Marianne held him tightly. 'It's not entirely the end, Oliver, we will meet again, but we have others to help too. We will never be far away; our world is very near, and who knows what assignments your Heavenly Father will appoint for us in future. It could easily happen that we'll all work together in helping others sometime. Think of it positively and not negatively. You all have your new lives to live, and the Father has many exciting things lined up for you.'

With that, they all embraced each other and said their goodbyes, and before anyone could say anything more, the family were on their own – the three messengers had vanished before their eyes. So the four of them mounted the stairs and said goodnight to each other on the landing. It was not very long until they climbed into bed. Despite the excitement of the day, all of them were soon soundly sleeping. That night there were no dreams and no disturbances – in fact, it was the best night's sleep they had had in years.

14. New Beginnings

Oliver woke quite early next morning, and as his eyes adjusted to the light streaming in through a gap in the curtains, he just couldn't believe his eyes. No longer was he in his bed in his room in *that* house, but rather he found himself in the house that had followed them throughout their wanderings – in the room that was complete with an en suite. His immediate thought was that all the experiences of the previous day had been part of an elaborate dream, and therefore in reality he and Jess were still pursuing the quest. He lay there for some time, puzzling as to how it could have been so real, yet here he was back in the other house.

A thought came to him and he jumped out of bed and rushed to the window: the house was not, as they'd come to expect, located in an open grassy space, but was in fact part of a row of houses that looked as though it was set on a housing estate. There was a beautiful garden with neatly trimmed hedges; beyond, he could see a few neighbours, one of whom was cleaning his car. This was no temporary home, this was a house permanently located in a very attractive area – everywhere looked clean, tidy and well maintained. Clearly, they had been relocated and the house was part of the relocation package.

He was so excited that he just had to go and find someone with whom to share the news. He went out onto the landing, but it seemed no one else was up yet, and everywhere was silent. After a time considering what to do, he decided to see if Jess was awake and so walked quietly to her door and knocked. There was no response so he knocked again; this time there was a very sleepy and muffled 'Hello?' from within, so Oliver opened the door slightly and spoke through the gap: 'Jess, are you awake?'

'Huh, I am now, because someone came knocking at my door – what time is it, anyway?'

'It's 6.45,' he responded. 'Sorry to disturb you.'

'6.45! You've got to be joking. Why are you up and about at this time?'

'Have you seen where you are? Have you seen what's happened during the night?'

'I haven't seen anything yet and neither will I, my eyes are still firmly shut and are not yet ready to face a new day. Anyway, what are you on about?'

'Open an eye and have a look around – what do you see?'

'Aargh, you're cruel to me, Olly! Just wait a bit, my eyes refuse to cooperate.' She finally declared, 'There, I've rubbed them and I think I've coaxed them into submission – so, I'm in my room, what am I supposed to see?'

'But what room – what room and what house?'

'Oh, that's too much for my little brain to take in at the moment: my room is in that… no, I'm not in that house, I'm in the other house, the one from our travels. How can that be? So are we back on our travels? I thought we'd arrived at our destination?'

'Take a look out the window. I reckon this is our ultimate destination and we've been relocated – see what you think, because we're not just plonked in an open space as we have been before, we're actually on an estate, I think. This, unless I'm mistaken, is our new home in a new town. They said we were having a completely new beginning and this is it – this is where it all starts.'

Oliver peered round the door just in time to see Jess struggling to the window, still trying to rub sleep from her eyes. As she looked, she gave a big 'Whoop!' and said, 'I reckon you're right! Wow, this looks great, this beats squats hands down! It looks better than anywhere I've lived before. So, do you think this house is our permanent new home? If it is, it's fantastic! I wonder if Mum and Dad have seen it yet.'

All the excitement and commotion brought very sleepy-looking parents out onto the landing to see what was going on. They came into Jess' room. 'What is it with you two, couldn't you sleep? What's all the fuss about?' their mum asked.

'Mum, Dad, get your eyes properly open, look around you, has anything changed?' Jess demanded.

'What do you mean "changed" – what's changed?' Jenny questioned.

'Er… Jen, take a good look,' said their Dad. 'They're right, everything's changed – this is a different house and yet we're all in it and it must have happened as we slept. Come to think of it, that's why I didn't immediately notice. I've been in this house before when Joshua was with me and I slept in the single bed I was in last night. Didn't you use it too when Marianne was with you, Jen?'

'You know, I believe you're right, and if that's the case, the bedroom has an en suite. I didn't have time to notice when we rushed from our room to see what all the excitement was about, and my eyes were hardly open anyway. So where are we? Are we in an open field somewhere?'

'No, that's just the point, Mum,' Oliver responded. 'It looks as though we're on a housing estate and this is our permanent home. Brilliant, isn't it? Although what town we're in, I don't know. It looks a nice area – look out of the window and you'll see for yourself.'

Peter and Jenny went to Jess' window to look out. 'Pete, this is great, don't you think? We can certainly make a new life for ourselves here.'

Peter threw an arm round her waist, drew her to him, lifted her chin and they kissed tenderly.

Jess gave a little cough. 'Er… excuse me, don't mind us, you two lovebirds.'

'We don't,' responded Peter with a laugh. 'We've got a lot of catching up to do. Anyway, back to the present. I think I know where we are.'

Everyone looked at him in surprise, waiting for his revelation. 'Think back to the early days, Jen, even before these two came on the scene. Where did we say that one day we were going to live, if given the opportunity?'

Jenny shook her head slowly as she tried to remember, but then a smile crossed her face. 'You mean Cornwall… St Glebes! You really think this is St Glebes?'

'I'm positive it is – it just has that feel and I can smell the sea. We'll go and explore after breakfast and see for certain if it is.'

'So what's so special about St Glebes?' Oliver asked. 'Have you been here before? Because we both felt it was sort of familiar to us – I thought it was a bit like Grandma's house?'

'No, if Dad's right, you haven't been here before. However, I know exactly what you mean, it does look like Grandma's house. It hadn't occurred to me before – I guess it must have been built to the same plans.'

'So where are we?' Jess asked.

'It's a lovely Cornish town where Dad and I spent our honeymoon. It's near to the sea and surrounded by beauty spots and places to visit – one lovely place is the Eden Project. Have you both heard of it?'

Jess shook her head, but Oliver said, 'I think a teacher once said something about it – big domed greenhouses and all sorts of exotic plants. I didn't hear much of what she was telling us, 'cause Jimmy Arnott was pinching me and kicking me at the time and others were flicking paper pellets at me.'

'I didn't know about all that,' said his mum. 'Why didn't you tell me? I'd have gone to the school and complained.'

'No, Mum, you know that couldn't have happened – that brute stood between us. But it's in the past now. Let's try to put it behind us and move on.'

Jenny grabbed Oliver and held him tightly. 'Sorry,' she whispered, and then added, 'I think you'll both enjoy being here if it is indeed St Glebes, it really does have a lot going for it.'

With that, they all went back to their rooms to prepare for the day, before going down for breakfast. Everything about the house was exactly as they remembered it, except that now it was back to reality – they discovered they had to prepare food themselves, no more automatic supplies!

They found a note awaiting them on the dining table. It read:

To you, our dear friends,

Greetings in that precious Name. We hope the change of accommodation was not too big a shock for you when you awoke this morning, and it is our hope that you will enjoy this new home (probably familiar to you all). The proceeds from the sale of your old house, Jenny, and your flat, Peter, have paid for it – it's yours. You will find the deeds, together with the remainder, deposited with your bank. All your possessions are here and positioned as close as possible to where you had things before. We've installed a few additional donated furnishings, which we think you'll enjoy.

We believe you had a long-standing desire to live in St Glebes and feel sure relocation here will cause you no regrets. There are local shops nearby and schools are only a short distance away.

You will be planning to explore this morning, and while you are doing so, you will meet with a couple in the marketplace who will ask if they can share something with you. They will invite you for refreshments in a café nearby. Go with them, because they will help you to belong in the local community of believers. That couple will also introduce you, Peter, to a Christian executive who is looking for someone with your skills.

Oliver and Jess, we have not forgotten you: you will meet a lovely couple who are church youth workers and they will introduce you to other young people. Great things will follow.

One other thing, there is a car in the garage that has been donated by someone who simply wants to bless you and welcome you. The keys and paperwork are in the drawer in the sideboard; you will need to transfer ownership, but it is already taxed and the MOT is not required for another year.

May blessings abound as you step into the future together. Thank you for being such a delight to know.

Your servants in Him,

Marianne, Joshua & Gabriel

No one could speak for quite some time; the contents of the letter had stunned them to silence. It was unbelievable; nothing, it seemed, had been overlooked and folk were being so generous. They had a lovely warm feeling inside and a sense of excitement as they anticipated the appointments they were going to have that day.

'Well, that confirms it, this is St Glebes,' said Peter, 'so that's our dream fulfilled, Jen; it's been a long time coming, but I'm sure it's perfect timing – something we all need and will benefit from. The past is exactly that: done, gone and never to rear its ugly head again. We may have to work through a few things, but we're all stronger now, and I reckon that, with help, we can do it. What do you think?'

'Yes, I'm sure. We needed this new start, and we now have a Helper to go with it.'

After breakfast, they set off to explore. Jenny and Peter were fully expecting St Glebes to have changed since they'd honeymooned there many years before. Where their house was located was very unfamiliar territory. As they walked down the street, they encountered neighbours, all of whom welcomed them to the area. The man next door asked when they'd moved in, as the house had been empty for some time and even the previous evening he thought it was still empty, so he was very surprised to see it wasn't. He went on to say that they must have been very quiet, as he had not even heard the removal van! They didn't feel they could explain as they didn't want him to think they were a bit crazy, so they all just smiled – reasoning that perhaps they could explain in due course once people got to know them.

It was a comparatively small estate and soon they emerged onto the main road that led into town. They window-shopped for a while and then decided to head towards the sea, but as they passed through the marketplace a couple approached them.

'Excuse us accosting you like this, but are you by any chance the Carrick family?'

'We are,' Peter answered. 'Peter and Jenny… and our children, Jess and Oliver. Do we know you?'

'No, you don't know us, but I think you know about us. I believe you were told to expect a couple to approach you and tell you that they had something to share with you, is that right?'

Peter confirmed that it was so and the couple then suggested that they all go to a local coffee shop to sit and talk. They were an amiable couple and the family were immediately at ease with them, so they were able to talk freely together. The couple introduced themselves as Tom and Heather Mills and said they were from the local Community Church.

'So how did you know about us?' asked Jess.

Heather answered, 'About a week ago we were praying together and we both heard the name "Carrick". It meant nothing to us; we have no one in our community by the name of Carrick, so we asked the Lord to reveal to us if this was a message from Him, and He said we'd meet with the four of you in the marketplace today. We've had similar experiences in the past and they've always proved genuine, so here we are.'

'Wow, that's fantastic,' Jenny responded, 'but were you told why you had to meet us?'

'Well…' Tom responded hesitantly. 'Am I right in thinking that you've all been on strange journeys and have also had some spiritual experiences?'

Oliver responded enthusiastically. 'We most certainly have, and an absolutely incredible journey it was too. On the way, we had some lovely people to teach us and encourage us. And now we're all together again after years apart! I think you can say God has been doing great things with us – we've even got a new house in a new town. Does that answer your question?'

Everyone was laughing, because all the time Oliver had been speaking he'd become more and more animated.

'In no uncertain terms, Oliver,' laughed Tom. 'Thank you. Your enthusiasm is infectious. Jess and Oliver, there's another couple who desperately want to meet you,' he continued. 'Sarah and Jack Mountford, who are our youth-work leaders. They would like you to join them for a meal on Friday evening at about 5.30pm and then go along with them to the youth meeting afterwards. They're a great couple and I think you'll get on well with them. Friday night is a fun evening and you'll find all sorts happening: it is a pretty good night. Would you be up for that? It would be a good opportunity to get to know other young people, many of whom you will no doubt be at school with.'

'Wow, that's kind of them,' Jess responded. 'They don't even know us, and yet they want to meet us! I'm certainly up for it. The quicker we can get to know people, the better. Where do they live?'

'This is their address,' said Tom, handing them a card. 'They asked us to pass it to you. They'll expect you unless they hear from you to the contrary. Jenny, you're not forgotten – I believe someone is going to contact you. They'll explain all!'

'By the way,' Heather added, 'you are under no obligation to join the Community Church if you don't feel it's for you, there is no pressure whatsoever, but it is our sincere hope that you will choose to join us. So now we'll leave you to explore.'

They parted and the family continued on their route towards the seafront, still totally bewildered by all they had just been told. St Glebes was even more beautiful than Peter and Jenny remembered it; on their journey, they saw St Glebes Community Church. It was a very attractive modern-looking building and they went to look at it more closely. The door was open and so they went inside; the interior was bright and felt welcoming.

They were just about to leave when a voice spoke from behind them. 'Hi there, can I help you at all?'

They turned and found a man casually dressed in shorts and a T-shirt and assumed that he was probably a caretaker.

'Oh, hi,' responded Peter, a little taken aback by the sudden appearance. 'We're new to the area and we're just exploring and we came across this church. We met a couple from here in the town, Tom and Heather. Do you know them?"

'Tom and Heather Mills? Yes, I know them, all right! Excuse me asking, you are not by any chance the Carrick family, are you?'

'Yes, that's us,' Peter responded. 'This is Jenny, my wife, Jess, our daughter, Oliver, our son, and I'm Peter. Are you the caretaker?'

The man laughed aloud before responding, 'I've been called many things but that's not one of them! Still, it is an apt description, because I take care of people – I'm the minister, Jim Partridge.'

'So… so sorry!' Peter stuttered. 'I hope I didn't offend you.'

'Offend me? Not in the least. I am so delighted to meet you all. Anyway, are you free this evening? Because if you are, I'd like to invite you to join us for a barbecue at, say, 6.30pm. Would that be possible, as I know my wife and family would love to meet all of you?'

'Fantastic, thank you for your kind offer; we've nothing planned, so I think we would love to join you. Where do you live?' asked Jenny

Jim Partridge led them outside and pointed to a nearby house. 'We live just there, so we'll see you all later – come just as you are; we're very informal.'

'I don't know about all of you,' said Peter, as they walked away, 'but I sort of feel we've come home, and this is where we really live, where we truly belong. Amazingly, the people here seem to know more about us than we know about ourselves. I think I'd quite like to try this church, which is perhaps only right, because they've gone out of their way to welcome us.'

Their visit to the minister's house that evening was a most enjoyable occasion, far better than they could ever have anticipated. The welcome they received immediately put them at their ease. The minister's wife, Helen, and Jenny immediately hit it off, and Peter assisted Jim with the barbecue; he and Jim had an instant rapport and chatted like old friends. Oliver and Jess were in their element, because the children, Jamie and Naomi, were of a similar age to them, so they immediately disappeared off together and played tennis on the lawn, using two chairs and a rope for a net. They chatted amiably as they played, until Jim shouted to them that dinner was ready. They didn't need telling twice! They all loved barbecues and they were hungry.

The rest of the evening was a most enjoyable time and established friendships that were destined to continue for years to come. Eventually all the children attended the same school and their circle of friends increased and became firmly established.

Over the days that followed things moved apace. Peter found a good job as head of finance in a local business. Jess and Oliver were enrolled in school, a move that Jess was unsure about as it was such a long time since she was in education last. In the event both of them were completely at ease and were welcomed by the other students, greatly helped by Jamie and Naomi. Jess, even with the aid of additional one-to-one tuition, had a lot of work to do, but she was patient and a quick learner. Without the bullying, Oliver even enjoyed being at school and made excellent progress.

Before she had married Peter and started the family, Jenny had been a nurse, but her years away meant that she was unable to slip back into it easily. Then one day, as predicted, someone spoke to her at church: 'I understand you used to be a nurse? I was told to approach you regarding a vacancy for a part-time nurse at the local hospice. Would you consider it, please?'

This resonated with Jenny and she knew immediately that it was her calling. She also knew she needed to retrain, so she enrolled in a refresher course and at the end of it joined the staff at the hospice. Caring for the terminally ill was a job she loved, and although it could be distressing when someone died, she knew she was making a big difference to the patients' final days.

Whenever they looked back to where they were just a few months earlier and where they now were, none of them ceased to give thanks to their Heavenly Father who had recognised their desperate plight and sent those guiding angels to help them. Those heavenly beings had stepped in to initiate the fantastic changes that had been fashioned in each of them. This had made it possible for healing and reconciliation to begin in their broken lives. It was nothing short of a miracle and none of them would ever be the same again.